A Scent of Roses

Helen Cannam is the author of more than twenty published works of fiction, most of which are now available in ebook form. For many years she lived on the edge of Weardale, where 'A Scent of Roses' is set. She now lives in Durham city.

A Scent of Roses

Helen Cannam

All situations and characters in this novel are
fictitious and any resemblance to any living person
is purely coincidental

Chapter One

He wasn't there. After all this, there was nothing.

Juliet had emptied the last of the kitchen packing cases, rubbed soiled hands on her dusty jeans and now stood back to look at the room. Overhead, the solid beams—scarred, dark with age—held hooks on which once herbs or hams or pots had hung, where one day she hoped they'd hang again. The oak dresser, bought at auction, had their decorative plates ranged on it, the ones that had lain unused for years after they'd inherited them from Leo's grandmother, waiting for just such a place to display them. A brand new Aga sent gleaming warmth into the room, though it unnerved her: she wasn't used to it yet. Over the sink, deep-set windows, stone-mullioned, looked out on a stretch of long grass to the wall that enclosed an overgrown orchard and a patch of weeds that had once been a garden, though whether of flowers or vegetables there was no telling now.

It was a beautiful room, an archetypal farmhouse kitchen, dim with greenish light, high-ceilinged, unevenly flagged, the Aga framed by the huge stone arch of an ancient fireplace, the sort that cried out for a settle to give it a finishing touch. They'd look out for one, Leo had promised.

Their home: a new home far away from the small regency house in Chelsea which they'd sold for three times what they'd paid for this place, giving them more than enough to fund the renovation, offering them a fresh start away from the painful memories, a chance to renew their lives, their marriage.

Only it didn't feel like home. Even with their things on the shelves and in the cupboards it felt empty, alien even. When they'd first seen it on a bright warm day in April, Juliet had for the first time in more than a year felt excitement and hope, which had remained in some measure right up to the moment a few days ago when they'd driven behind the removal van to their new front door; which was in fact the back door, leading from the cobbled farmyard to the passage that led into the kitchen. But she had no sense of excitement now nor of hope, only weariness and a stark loneliness. Then, the two of them had wanted to leave the past behind. Now she knew that she did not after all want to cut herself off from it so completely. In London she had felt that everything fed her grief. Now, paradoxically, the grief seemed worse because there was nothing to feed it.

Luke wasn't here. There was no sense of him left, nothing at all. She did not even feel as if she'd carried anything of him with her. She had never felt so alone, utterly cut off from all that she had been, all she was, everything she cared about. In London it had been painful beyond words, beyond imagining, to be reminded of him at every turn, in every fall of a curtain, every angle of light through a window, every small thing—a mug he'd drunk from, a note of music he'd loved (or hated), a door opening as if he were about to walk through it —but *not* to be reminded was worse. She ached for him, longed for him with every one of her senses.

She could hear Leo banging around somewhere in the further reaches of the house, removing cracked plaster perhaps (there was a lot of that), or dealing with the leaking tap in the bathroom. Now she'd done what she could in the kitchen, she ought to go and see if she could help him. It was what they'd planned, to work together on this place. And he at least was the one constant with their old life, the one thing that had come with her from the past. Only there was no companionship there, no solace, had not been for so long now. They had come here to try to rediscover the link that had been severed so brutally on that April day nineteen months ago—16 April 2006, a date scarred on her memory. But now, at this moment, she thought they must have been insane to think they could do it, simply by moving house, taking on a new joint project.

And if it were somehow possible, was that even what she wanted any more?

Stupid question! There was only one thing she really wanted, and that she could never have; never, never…

Her eyes misted with tears, the too-familiar obstruction rose in her throat. She must get out of here, get some fresh air! Abruptly, she pulled on the old blue fleece that lay over the back of one of the kitchen chairs and went outside, into the late afternoon sunshine.

She crossed the grass—you could hardly call it a lawn yet, though it shouldn't be too difficult to get it back into some sort of order—and made for the rickety wooden gate in the stone wall beyond. Once there, she forced it open, taking care not to allow it to fall apart completely, propped it wide and then stood there, gazing out over the tangle of weeds, taking in the utter tranquillity of the place; the absence of traffic noise, sirens, feet clattering on pavements—just birdsong and the wind stirring the trees. The light was clear, bright, intense, the distant hills deeply purple and blue; the surrounding wall (what she could see of it through the brambles and grass) gold, lichen-silver, green, like the branches of the ancient apple trees, whose gnarled shapes were picked out with extraordinary clarity. The air, carried to her straight from the hills on the lightest of breezes, was fragrant with moorland scents.

Breathing deeply, she pushed her way along what must once have been a path. a line running directly ahead of her, still faintly visible if only as a scarcely perceptible difference in the shade of green. Confronted soon with a more than usually vigorous bramble, she halted again. It was so warm here, the air soft—and a new scent reached her now, a heady domesticated perfume, strong, musky: old roses. Somewhere in that tangle of growth there must be an old rose still in bloom even so late in the season. She looked about her for what the scent brought to mind—the folded petals, crimson, pink, the colours that were the essence of rose.

She couldn't see it. The scent was stronger than ever as she stooped, parting the fronds of grass, the harsh scratching brambles. But still she could see no sign of it. There was blood on her hands—it was impossible to avoid the thorns, but they weren't from roses, or none that she could see. In all this lavish growth she could find only weeds. Yet the scent was so concentrated, filling her senses. The rose must be somewhere round here and in bloom otherwise there would have been no scent. She must find it! A rose so sweet should not be lost, not choked by weeds. She would give it space to breathe, cherish it, nurture it, take cuttings if need be so that the garden would be filled with its perfume—as it was filled now. Strange, when she'd still found nothing else to indicate the presence of the rose...

'What are you doing?'

She turned to see Leo watching her from just outside the gate. 'Looking for a rose. The one you can smell.'

'I can't smell anything.'

'Come over here. It's beautiful.'

'If you think I'm going to get myself scratched to pieces you can think again. I shouldn't think a rose would stand a chance in there.'

'That's why I must find it.' With sudden resolution, she made her way to where Leo was standing. 'Where did we put the gardening things?'

'The first outhouse from the back door.

You're surely not going to start on it now?'

'Why not?'

'Well, for one thing it's half past seven. I was going to suggest we tried that pub in the village, near the library. *King's Head*; *Queen's Arms*—something like that. You know the one.'

'Just half an hour. Just give me time to uncover it.'

'Leave it, Juliet. Let it rest.' His voice was gentle, intended to be soothing, though it did not soothe, had not been able to since—oh, for months now, more than a year.

She looked at him, at the stubborn set of his mouth. So like Luke's mouth, when he wanted something and was determined to have it no matter what. That car, for instance—

In a way Leo was now all she had left of Luke, because Luke had been so like him in so many ways—looks, mannerisms, temperament. Sometimes she'd resented the fact that there was so little of her in their son; found it an added grief when in all her anger with Leo she still couldn't fail to see Luke in him. She'd wanted to push him away, but in doing so she knew she'd lose that link with their son, so she'd stayed and tried to hold on to their marriage. It was the one single tenuous thing that had kept them together as far as she was concerned. It had brought them here. But would it take them on together into the future? Sometimes she doubted it.

Feeling suddenly overwhelmingly tired, she gave in, pushed her way back through the brambles, closed the gate as far as it would go—there wasn't anything to be kept out anyway, nor anything in need of protection—and came alongside her husband. 'OK. Let's go eat.'

Meadhope was, in places, a pretty village. It had an ugly scar of a red-brick council estate, a scattering of factories, some now derelict, and the usual featureless modern developments on its fringes. But at its heart were clusters of stone cottages, a fine old church and several inviting-looking pubs.

Appearances were deceptive. The *Royal Oak* was not a success. Warm and friendly, yes, with a buzz of happy chatter, though from people who seemed depressingly unlike the company they were used to. Juliet looked about her at the largely elderly clientele, all fine-knit sweaters and elasticated waistbands—no wonder about the latter, for the food when it came was piled high on massive plates, more than either of them could eat; had it been edible, that is.

Overcooked, the vegetables were clearly freezer-to-microwave, the meat some packaged stuff of indeterminate origin, smothered in gravy made from powder, luridly coloured, over-salty. It was an uncomfortable meal not just because of the food but because, as usual, they had little to say to one another, eating in a silence heavy with things that could not be said; though as they left Leo's comment was: 'Let's hope that's not the best this place has to offer, or I'm going back to London.' He meant it as a joke, but Juliet was not so sure. Had they made a terrible mistake in coming here?

Back at home, they said goodnight to one another, politely, on the landing at the head of the main stairs, and went to their separate beds, Leo to the single divan in his study, Juliet to the king-sized bed in the master bedroom above the passage that divided the later part of the house from its ancient origins. For many years now they'd slept in separate rooms, because Leo's snoring kept Juliet awake. Before Luke's death, that had not inhibited them from enjoying a full and mutually satisfying sex life, which had sustained their relationship even when Leo was too bound up in his work to take much part in family life. As in so many other ways, Luke's death had changed all that. For months afterwards, the debilitating inertia of grief had wiped out any inclination Juliet might have had towards intimacy. When desire returned, it was as a simple physical need, satisfied, so far as it went, by the angry urgency of the two occasions when she and Leo had gone to bed together. Once only had they rediscovered anything approaching the passion and tenderness of their old relationship, and that had been on the night they'd heard Holywell was theirs. It had not lasted.

At the door of her room, Juliet hesitated. Why not tonight? It had been a long time. They were on the verge of a new life together...'Leo!'

He turned to look at her, the curve of his mouth, the questioning tilt of his dark brow suddenly so like Luke's that she felt a savage stab of pain. Desire shrivelled and died.

'Goodnight,' she said.

In her room, with the soft sound of the wind in the trees the only disturbance, she was glad to be alone. What with the fresh air and the exertion of unpacking, she was achingly tired. Once in bed, she dropped asleep almost at once, deeply, peacefully, as she had not done for a very long time. She had a dream too, and not this time one of those dreams of Luke alive and well from which she would wake to the agonising realisation that the nightmare was real and he had gone for ever.

This time, she found herself looking down on the garden and there, where she had caught the scent of roses, stood a woman. She was slight, dark and dressed in some sort of long stiff black garment, a bit like a woman in one of those seventeenth century Dutch interior paintings, with a starched cartwheel of a ruff at her neck and a close-fitting hood on the back of her head. All around her in a pattern of small formal beds edged with low box hedging were roses, lovely old shrub roses in crimson and blush-pink, some streaked with white. She bent down towards one of the flowers and, with eyes closed, slowly breathed in the scent; then she straightened, turned, and seemed to look directly at Juliet with her glowing dark eyes. There was warmth in them, understanding, a kind of wordless reaching out in friendship; and something more.

Juliet woke to the first grey light of dawn and an unexpected feeling of solace. What a strange dream! So vivid and so detailed, as if it had been absolutely real—she could remember everything about it with the utmost clarity, as if it had actually, really happened to her, just a moment before. There was nothing especially remarkable in dreaming about the garden after what had happened yesterday, but this seemed almost like a direct message to her, an urgent plea to restore it to what it once had been.

Suddenly invigorated, she leapt out of bed, dressed in old clothes and slipped down the back stairs, out to the yard and the shed where the garden tools were kept. In a soft drizzly rain, Juliet set to work on the garden, in the very place where the rose perfume was strongest; even now, though fainter, it was clearly discernible. She dragged out brambles and nettles, covering her arms with stings and scratches; pulled at ground elder, cut back small trees that had seeded themselves everywhere (she'd leave the heavy digging until later), ripped out every weed she could see, everything that was not a rose. By the time the rain had ceased and a faint watery sun was in the sky she'd cleared the centre of the garden, if only roughly, from wall to wall. She stood up, with the scent of roses still heavy in her nostrils, and looked about her. There was nothing, no sign at all of any rose, not even a struggling remnant of an ancient shrub. How was that possible? Where on earth was the scent coming from?

Leo, a mug of coffee in his hand, found her like that. 'What's got into you, Juliet? This is mad! You don't even like gardening.'

'I can't find the rose.'

He pushed open the gate and came towards her. 'What rose?'

'The one you can smell. I told you! The most lovely scent.'

He sniffed, vigorously. 'I can't smell anything.'

'But you must! It's really strong!'

'Not to me it isn't.'

This was the man who prided himself on a nose so sensitive it could detect which grapes had been used in the making of a wine—'Try again!'

He did, with the same result. By now he was growing impatient. 'For goodness sake, Juliet, you're becoming obsessed! You haven't even had breakfast yet, have you? Leave this for now. I thought we were going to let it lie for a year and see what came up. And then get a garden designer to give it a makeover. Anything rather than do it ourselves. We've got quite enough to do as it is.'

'But I can smell it—' She caught his expression, exasperated and sceptical. She wondered whether to tell him about her dream, but decided against it. On first waking, she had thought it significant, a dream containing a message; now it seemed just a dream—or would have done had it not been for the scent. 'All right, I'll leave it for now. I'm not giving up though.'

Later that day, when she walked over the cleared garden, she could smell nothing but newly-turned earth. She felt ridiculously disappointed.

Chapter Two

Last night, she'd been in Juliet's dreams again: the lady in the garden, walking along the grassy paths, once more turning to smile at her, with approval, in friendship. Somehow she'd seemed to say, *You're not alone here. I am your companion in this place, a benign spirit, for I too once lived here and loved it. Here is my garden, which I know you will restore to new life.*

Propelled from her bed by an unfamiliar burst of optimism, Juliet had been eager to work on the garden again this morning—the rose might still be there after all—but when, over breakfast, she'd hinted at the possibility, Leo had frowned. 'We've enough to do indoors. If you waste time in the garden we'll never get the house fit to live in.'

So, in the face of his disapproval, she had gone instead to the room set aside as her office and begun to unpack the few things for which she could find a place. Having arranged her photographs of Luke on the table she used as a desk, she was gazing at them as if by looking and longing she could somehow make them come to life, when something caught her eye: on the surface near them was a rough scratch, just one of many marks that age and use had left on the once-polished oak. Except that it was not 'just one more mark', not to her, who remembered five-year-old Luke reaching for the paper-knife she kept in a drawer and, proud of his newly-acquired ability to shape the letters, starting to inscribe his name in the wood. She'd been furious at the time—the desk had been new, its surface pristine, glossy, unmarked. Now she ran her fingers over the old scar—a rough L shape, the first curve of the U—and felt that it was the best thing about it. She did after all still have some small tangible memento of her son, here in this place that was hers alone; and of course there was the box in which she'd packed all his lovingly accumulated offerings: clumsy handmade Mothers' Day cards, lopsided papiermâché models, postcards sent home from school trips abroad. The painful sense of having left everything behind, of having cut herself off from the past—that was suddenly swept away. Luke *was* here, and with him she had her lady in the garden, the tutelary spirit of this place, to watch over and encourage her. In an odd way she felt as if those two things were somehow connected, as if the lady in her dream had been instrumental in drawing her attention to the indentations her fingers were tracing.

'Juliet! Come and look at this!' It was a moment or two before she realised that Leo was calling her from the foot of the stairs.

What now? 'I'm in the middle of something!' In the midst of memories, of finding a brief moment of consolation…But it had gone now, flown from her in an instant, restoring her to the brutal reality of the present.

'Leave it. This is important!'

With a sigh she made her way down to where Leo stood at the foot of the stairs. For the first time in more than two years she'd been filled with something that was almost like happiness, marred only because she had no one to talk to about it—about the garden, the lady, the scar on her desk. She knew she couldn't share it with Leo, because she could no longer talk to him about anything that mattered. And he'd made things worse by interrupting her reverie.

As her gaze focussed on Leo's face, she saw that it was alight with excitement. 'Come and see what I've found!' He led the way outside, along the yard to the first of the outbuildings that faced onto it. 'I was looking to see what was in that heap of old machinery in here, and happened to shift a few things. And—' He pushed open the door, so that dim light fell on the wall to their left. 'See, there! What do you think that is?'

From where she stood Juliet could make out a bulge at the far end of the stone wall, a uniform roundness up to what would have been first floor level, had there been a first floor in this high raftered barn. She shivered, though quite why she did not know, except that she felt suddenly uneasy.

'A sort of little turret—?'

'Could be. Except that it doesn't go up to the roof, and I doubt if it ever has. You know what I think?' She shook her head. 'It's my guess there's been a spiral stair there at some time.'

Suppressing an inexplicable urge to run away—what was the matter with her?—Juliet said, 'But where would it go to? There aren't any rooms up there.'

'I guess there would have been once—late mediaeval perhaps. They'll have wanted more privacy than the hall gave, in the days when there was just the hall to live in—so they'd have built a solar, a sort of sitting room, and maybe some bedrooms too. They probably fell into disrepair and were demolished when they built the byre. I think there was probably once a room over the hall too. Anyway, come and have a look inside.'

He led the way back into the house *(thank goodness!)*, through the kitchen and its adjoining rooms, across the central passage that linked front and back doors and pushed open the heavy oak door that closed off the ancient hall from the rest of the house. 'Look what I found in here!'

She was filled with an extraordinary sense of reluctance. She did not want to go any further. In fact, her overwhelming instinct was to retreat, pushing the door closed behind her.

'Juliet?' Leo sounded puzzled.

What was the matter with her? She looked around, in case some instinct was warning her about an unsafe roof or wall. They already knew, from their surveyor's report, that the hall needed major repairs. She could see nothing out of the ordinary, yet her heart was thudding with growing panic.

With a massive effort she took a deep breath and forced herself to cross the room to where Leo stood. He grinned at her, full of boyish excitement, and gestured towards the far corner. 'That's where the spiral stairs are, if they are spiral stairs—on the other side of that wall. I've done some investigating.'

She saw then that in one place the rough plaster—it was the only plastered wall in the room—had been partially chipped away, revealing red bricks, incongruous against the ancient stone of the rest of the room, and also: 'See, this—part of an arch. There was a doorway here once, I'm sure of it—the door to the spiral stairs!' He ran his hand over the curve of finely dressed stone, with all the eager excitement of a boy unwrapping a longed-for present. 'We've got to open it up. It'll make a wonderful feature. You can see that, I'm sure, with your designer's eye.'

Juliet felt herself swept by a wave of repulsion that amounted almost to horror. She wanted to say, *'No! Leave it alone! Cover it up again!'* but she didn't. Leo would find such a reaction utterly bewildering; naturally enough, since she couldn't understand it herself. What was it about this place—or about her? 'We'd have to get listed building consent. Haven't we got enough in the pipeline already?'

'Oh they'd have no objections, with something so old. I'm sure of that. Probably be delighted that we're prepared to restore something so significant.'

'Haven't we got enough to do?' *Don't do it! Don't do it!* Screamed a voice in her head. *Leave it alone!*

'But this is exceptional! We've already got the go-ahead to take the plaster off and repoint the stonework. You wouldn't want that ugly red brick infill left there would you?'

'Can't we just replaster it? It'll be warmer plastered.'

'And cover over that fine arch? It would be vandalism! Besides, we've not got consent to replaster.'

'We haven't got full consent for anything yet.' She knew that was not what worried her, but she didn't know what it was that made her recoil from the very idea, to regret even the little Leo had done so far. 'It's cold in here. I'm getting back to my unpacking.'

'Well, I'm going get some more of that plaster off.' He could see that the resistance in her expression had not lessened in the least. 'I shall open it up—but I promise I'll fill it in again with decent stone if you really don't like it when it's done, or in the unlikely event that English Heritage tell us to. Just humour me in this one thing!' To her relief he moved back towards the door by which they'd come in. 'I don't suppose you want to give me a hand?'

She suppressed a shiver. 'I could do with some fresh air. I might go into Meadhope, have a look round.'

'Good idea. See if there's anywhere that looks more promising for eating out.'

As soon as she closed the door of the hall

behind her, Juliet felt restored to normal. The peace of the house enveloped her again, so that the unease she'd felt seemed a great fuss about nothing. All the same, a change of scene would be a good idea.

As she got ready to go out, she considered the house, the centuries that had passed since its first building; wondering about the people who had lived here in all that time, of whom they were simply the latest. Perhaps their coming here had not been the chance happening it had seemed, or even a matter of their own choosing, but something that was meant to be.

It had happened completely without warning, just after the first anniversary of Luke's death—and on the very day when Juliet had decided once and for all that she and Leo had no future together and that she must leave him. She had not quite reached the point of working out how she would do it or where she would go, only that she could no longer bear to go on living like this. There was somewhere in her mind an indistinct picture of a single simple room, stripped of all but the barest necessities, where she could hide like a wounded animal and shut out the world.

Yet—to tear herself from all that reminded her of Luke, in this house, these Chelsea streets, and in Leo himself, the sturdy brown-haired man who had fathered a younger copy of himself in the boy who had died—how could she bear to do that? Only because it might somehow be less painful than living day after day in the loneliness of their shattered relationship...

She'd heard Leo come in from work and gone to meet him in the hall, bracing herself to tell him of her decision—and then had been brought up short by an oddly feverish light in his eyes, a look of excitement such as she could not remember having seen before, and certainly not during the past year. He'd thrown his briefcase down on the hall floor (that was unusual in itself, for he was by nature the most tidy of men) and then come towards her with arms held out.

'Well, it's done! That's it. I'm leaving.'

She'd recoiled, stabbed by a sudden pain, her breath caught in her throat. That was the wrong way: she was the one who was about to leave, who had every justification for doing so. How could he leave her? How could he even want to?

Then she realised through the bewildered confusion of her feelings that he was smiling in a way that *included* her rather than shut her out.

From somewhere her voice croaked a question. 'Leaving?'

'My job. The City. Gainful employment. Money and long hours and big bonuses. I'm getting out. *We're* getting out.'

'We?'

'We'll move to the country. Find an old property in need of TLC. Do it up—our dream home. Do country things—oh, you'll know the kind of thing. Take up hunting, join the WI.'

She'd given a shaky laugh. 'Men don't usually—join the WI, I mean.' She'd stared at him, trying to make sense of it. 'You don't know anything about the country. You've never lived anywhere but London.'

'But you have. You've often said how much you miss the open spaces, riding, all those things.'

'That was years ago. You never agreed anyway.'

'Well, now I do. I want a complete change. Put the past behind us and try something completely new. How does that sound?'

In some strange way, his enthusiasm had something infectious about it that had reached her in spite of herself, though she'd tried hard to resist, was even aware of a surge of anger. He had suddenly walked in on her decision and thrown everything to the winds. And there was something unbalanced about the way he had done it, which made her doubly wary. Yet…

What did she really want? Was there a chance that their marriage might be salvaged after all? Could she wish for that, believe it possible? She had no idea. The only thing she'd really wanted for a long time was the thing she could never have: Luke back, alive and well.

Leo had gone to the wine rack in the kitchen and brought out a bottle of champagne. 'Let's celebrate. No more work for me, ever. Well, only real work, work with my hands. I can't wait.'

Was he really serious? Was this a passing mood, which would be gone in a day or two? Not if he had truly resigned from his job…

'Where will we go?'

'Wherever. Where we find the right place. No preconceptions, no fixed ideas—it's a time for impulse and instinct, not rational thought.'

'Isn't that what your job's been based on anyway? I didn't think there was that much rationality in the city. You said so yourself.'

'Ah, but the aims are rational, brutally so— make as much money as you can as quickly as possible, no matter how, no matter what the consequences. That's what I'm leaving behind. Now life will have a purpose, a real point that has nothing to do with making money.'

A purpose, without Luke? Was that possible? 'We've still got to eat.'

'Of course we have. Think what we'll get for this house in the current climate! Wisely invested, it should buy us a good country property and give us the means to do it up— and probably some left over too. And I can always do a bit of consultancy work on the side if need be. I'll have a good pension too, even if I don't take it yet. And it's not as if we haven't got some savings. You see, I've thought it all out.'

'How long have you been planning all this?' She'd had no idea, never for a moment dreamed of what was in his mind. He'd shown no sign of anything unusual—apart from the unexplained absences. Could they have had anything to do with it, rather than being, as she'd thought, the only manifestation of his grief?

'Oh, it's been brewing a good while. But I didn't want to say anything until I was sure.'

Once, he'd have confided in her long before doing anything so drastic as giving up his job; though she could never have imagined him ever wanting to do something so fundamentally out of character. But it was a very long time since they'd felt able to confide in one another, while the huge matter of the tangle of emotions about Luke's death remained unexamined, kept in, each of them maintaining silence, hiding their real feelings. Did Leo ever wonder what she felt or thought? Did he have any idea of her anger and pain? That day, looking at his excited face, she'd wondered if he'd put his memories of Luke behind him, along with his job and the past life he wanted to discard. Was that possible? How could she tell? It was as if she no longer knew him at all, this man who once had been her best friend, the love of her life.

She'd opened her mouth to say, 'But if we leave here, we leave all our memories behind, all the things to do with Luke.' But she didn't say it. After all, it was what she herself had been planning to do. Besides, she was afraid of what other things it might lead to, what a storm of emotion it might bring into the open.

She didn't want champagne either. It felt wrong, but she sipped at the drink, listened to Leo's excited talk, and then served the supper she'd prepared. She didn't want to say anything, to commit herself to anything, until she knew what she really thought about it all. For the time being she felt only disorientated, her emotions in turmoil.

Leo was up half the night scanning properties on the internet. She refused to look at what he'd found. 'It's your idea. I'm leaving it to you. Just tell me when you think you've found the place.'

'But you've got to like it too.'

'I'll tell you if I don't when you've found it.'

Which was how, one evening some days later, he came across Holywell. He'd printed off the details and brought them to her in the sitting room. 'I've found it! This has to be the one!'

She'd scanned the description: *Historic dales farmhouse...* looked at the pictures. It was undeniably beautiful, the soft pale honey-coloured stone, the tangled garden, the huge rooms, even the near-dereliction asking for their mark to be made upon it. She'd felt a tingle of excitement—and then looked at the address: *County Durham.* 'Leo, we can't go there. It's practically in Scotland. What's the betting it's surrounding by pit heaps? And it'll rain all the time.'

'Durham City's a fine place. It's not far from there.'

Where Luke should have gone, as a student —that was hardly designed to make her feel better about it all. Did he even recall that fact?

'We'll go and have a look at it,' he'd decided. 'If you're right, then no, we won't buy it. Simple!'

The sun had been shining when they first saw it; in fact it had been incredibly warm for late April. And there were no pit heaps, only a wide green valley dotted with stone farmhouses, and fields in which sheep and cattle grazed, and a village near enough to provide their most basic needs. They had fallen in love, both of them. As they got in the car at the end of the viewing they had looked at one another with a smiling intimacy they had not known for a very long time. 'Yes, you're right,' Juliet had said. 'This is it.'

Subsequent viewing in less clement weather had failed to change their minds. For the first time, she had begun to hope—to believe—that they might have a future, that life might become bearable again.

Yet today she was puzzling over the unease that had troubled her, faced with Leo's excitement—over a hidden stair, of all things! What was the matter with her?

Time to go out, time for some fresh air, she thought, and went to get her coat.

Fallen leaves fringed the lane with bronze.

Crushed under Juliet's shoes, their scent came up to her, sharp with the memory of Luke's conker-brown lace-ups kicking through leaves as she walked him to school. Such a sweet self-contained little person he'd been then, in his shorts and blazer, knee socks, striped cap pressed down on hair bright as his shoes; laughing, chattering—non-stop chatter. What had he talked about? If only she could remember, have it imprinted somewhere on her mind, instantly retrievable, like a CD she could play whenever she chose. But it had gone, leaving only its shadow, its echo. If ever she recalled any of his actual words, it was because they'd stayed in her mind, not as they had been at first, fresh from his mouth in the moment of utterance, but distanced by later repetition, when she'd told others about them, to amuse them or make them wonder at his precociousness, his infant wit.

Was it one occasion she recalled now, or many merged into one? Year after year she'd walked with him through leaves, under bare boughs, beneath falling blossom and new green foliage, until he grew too old to bear her company. Then she'd watched from the door as he walked away alone, gazing after him until he disappeared round the turn in the road. Foolish and sentimental, Leo had called her, soft for not being able to let him go; but now, looking back, she wished there had been more times, more years, when she'd savoured every moment that she'd been with him, every last sighting of him.

There was one autumn day that was clearer in her mind, she recalled suddenly. As they'd walked together he'd stopped to look at a car, a sports car parked at the roadside. Even then at —what?—six years old, he'd been excited by fast cars. She could still see his beatific smile as he gazed at it. Fool that she was, she'd been charmed by his joy. If she'd known, then—but it was just as well not to know. Except that if you realised in your bones how fragile life was to be, how little time you had left, then you would be sure to make the most of every second…

She followed the lane as it curved round towards Meadhope's ancient church, its graveyard bordered with trees golden with autumn. She'd bought herself a lunch of soup at a small café on the corner of the market place; quite good soup, she'd been agreeably surprised to find, with home-made bread warm from the oven. Then she'd decided to explore the winding back lanes of the village, where— here, now—memory had clutched at her, with its mixture of love and pain.

The lane emerged suddenly into another one, running at right angles to it. To the left, it seemed to lead back to the main street—she caught a distant glimpse of cars rushing by; to the right, it ran up to the church, ancient stone in an ancient churchyard. Just this side of the lychgate, a noticeboard stood propped by an opening in a wall. The name jumped out at her, *his* name: Luke. She felt stifled, choked.

Gradually, through the shock and pain that leapt in her, the rest of the words took shape and reached her: *St Luke's autumn fair, 1.30-4.00.* She could hear animated voices from just out of sight, so she followed the sound and found herself in a yard beside what was clearly the church hall. Well, she hadn't anything better to do and the name drew her. Why not go in?

Meadhope church hall was not really large enough to accommodate all the stalls for the autumn fair, so they were crammed closer together than was comfortable, since at this time of year there was no question of overflowing into the nearby rectory garden as they usually did (weather permitting) for the annual summer fête.

The Reverend Rosalind Maclaren, rector of Meadhope and the nearby hamlet of Ashburn, had been there for an hour or so, helping set out the stalls and then walking among them, offering assistance here and there and encouragement everywhere. She took a particularly long time at the Fair Trade stall, the only one whose proceeds would not be going to church funds. It had taken several heated sessions of the Parochial Church Council before its members had agreed to allow this innovation to the autumn sale, and there were still several of her parishioners who would never be reconciled to money going out of the parish. *Charity begins at home,* was a phrase she hated and had once never dreamed she would hear in any Christian context, only to be sadly disillusioned on far too many occasions. The two ladies in charge of the stall—Lisa Emerson, a young mother with a fiercely active social conscience, and 90-year-old retired headmistress Philippa Lee—were passionately opposed to such parochialism.

She wondered when Alastair would arrive. Her husband was bringing his mother along, so Rosalind was bracing herself to cope with Jessie's demands for attention, her total absence of any concession to Rosalind's role as rector of the parish, her insistence that it was her daughter-in-law's duty to put her first. It was not easy having her living so near to them, but it was preferable to trying to deal with the same demands at long distance, as had been the case when Jessie was still living in her native Scotland, to which she'd returned after her husband's death.

Rosalind paused by the cake stall, for which a stream of parishioners brought cakes of all kinds—butterfly buns, victoria sandwich cakes, fruit loaves, chocolate cakes oozing cream—and smiled to herself, knowing how Alastair would react when he saw them. There was one of Elsie Hope's famous lemon drizzle cakes. 'I'll put it by for you.' Jan Grey, in charge of the stall, knew Alastair's tastes very well by now.

An arm suddenly encircled Rosalind's shoulder. 'How about one of the chocolate cakes too?' asked her son Josh. She turned to look at him, reaching up to brush his cheek with her hand. He'd shaved today, which was a good sign: perhaps he was beginning to leave the worst behind him. Though she'd thought that before, only to have her hopes dashed. She knew well enough, with her long experience of such things—her own and others'—how slow a process was the recovery from bereavement, of any kind.

He still looked so thin and drawn, very

unlike the bright hopeful youth who had set out for Lesotho five years ago. She would have worried about his health, knowing how Miriam had died, had he not had that definitive barrage of tests. They'd been clear, every time, and she knew it was only grief. *Only*—!

'I thought you weren't going to come until after the opening?'

He pulled a wry face. 'Oh God, am I too early? I thought I'd timed it right.'

'Oh, just on cue! Here's Daphne Wynyard now.' Daphne Wynyard was the nearest the parish had to a lady of the manor, since her family had lived at Ashburn Hall for generations, as a consequence of which she had long been the default opener for all local functions, at least when no minor celebrity was available.

'She scrubs up well,' Josh murmured. Rosalind was too glad to hear him make a joke, however inappropriate, to do more than grin at him before going to greet Daphne. Josh was quite right: in honour of the occasion she had changed her everyday cord trousers and Barbour jacket for a surprisingly elegant blue wool dress, with pearls and matching handbag and shoes; she had even applied a modest amount of make-up and had her hair styled.

'Not late am I?' she asked, without waiting for a reply. 'Where do you want me? Up aloft?'

She mounted the stage while Rosalind called for silence; and opened proceedings with little more than a plea for everyone to spend lavishly in a good cause.

During the clapping that followed, Josh muttered, 'Better than that one you had that time—you know, from local radio. The one who went on about all the important things he'd done, for hours and hours.'

'A slight exaggeration, but I know the one you mean. He won't be asked back, for all he has a strong fan club in Meadhope. Or did have.' She stepped forward to thank Daphne, though by now the general hubbub of buying drowned her words.

At that moment she saw Alastair and his mother standing just inside the door. They came across the room, Jessie's long bony frame leaning heavily on her son's arm, though she had her walking stick in the other hand. There was a new bruise on her cheek—she must have had another of those sudden falls. *She's not getting any better...*Rosalind tried her best to banish the thought, while knowing that they'd have to face it sooner rather than later. But not today.

'It's a terrible crush,' Jessie greeted her when

they met, ignoring the welcoming smile and drawing back a little from her daughter-in-law's kiss. She was not a demonstrative woman.

Rosalind refrained (just) from pointing out that they had warned her what it would be like, but she'd insisted on coming. 'Perhaps you'd like a cup of tea. There are some lovely homemade biscuits.'

'I have just had my lunch.' As usual, her tone was that of someone rebuking a rather dim child who had failed to recognise the obvious. 'You can help me choose a little Christmas present for Daisy and Edith.' They were her great-granddaughters, children of Josh's older sister Sophie.

'I'm afraid Rosalind has other demands on her time just now, Mother.' Alastair steered her gently towards the craft stall, with its handmade garments and toys, leaving Rosalind to accompany Daphne on her official rounds of the hall; and then to circulate in general, pausing to ask after this person and that.

An hour later, the cake stall was empty and Jessie Maclaren had at last agreed to sit down and allow Alastair to bring her a cup of tea, where Josh had joined her and was listening patiently to her complaints about the crowds, the temperature, and the quality and prices of the goods on sale.

Rosalind had just bought a pink knitted coat that was probably already too small for one-year-old Edith, her youngest grandchild, but then very few people bought knitted garments for babies these days, however lovingly and skilfully made. 'This is sure to become a family heirloom,' she told Anita Carr, who, having knitted most of its produce herself, was feeling discouraged by the lack of interest in her stall. Alastair had once joked that Rosalind would probably save money simply by making a generous donation to church funds, rather than spending what she felt was necessary at the twice-yearly church sales. He had a point, except that Rosalind knew that most of the stall holders found real satisfaction in making things and selling them on behalf of the church. Money wasn't everything, even when it was for church funds.

'I wonder who that is?' Anita's attention was caught by someone at the other end of the hall. In a village where anyone who'd lived there for any length of time knew nearly everyone else, at least by sight, a complete stranger at a village event was a rarity.

A woman had just wandered in, pausing

inside the door to look about her. She was about her own age, Rosalind thought, perhaps a little older; dressed casually, but in the sort of elegant expensive casuals one rarely saw in Meadhope, an exquisite black and blue leather handbag clasped in one hand: definitely a high-maintenance lady. She began to walk the length of the hall, looking about her with a slightly dazed look, as if she wasn't quite sure how she came to find herself there. *I've not seen her before… Or have I?* wondered Rosalind. Certainly she had never seen her in Meadhope, or anywhere else she could think of. Yet there was something about her, something that stirred in Rosalind's memory at the way she turned her head, the polite, automatic smile as she paused at the tombola stall, looking at what was left but clearly unimpressed by the selection of cheap shower gel and sweet sparkling wine. She came on, approaching where Rosalind was standing. Then she looked directly at her—blue eyes under finely arched brows, exquisite high cheekbones (not perhaps entirely due to nature), ivory complexion. Yes, Rosalind had seen her before, or perhaps someone very like her. But who? And where?

It was clear now that the woman was thinking much the same. There was that look of almost-recognition in her eyes, the question clearly forming in her mind.

In the end they spoke at the same moment:

'Haven't we——?'

'I know you from somewhere, don't I?'

They both laughed; embarrassed yet intrigued. 'Rosalind Maclaren—I'm rector here.'

It was clear she hadn't answered the other woman's question, though she was continuing to search her memory for some connection. 'Juliet Marston. We've just moved to the area.'

Rosalind shook her head, then added, 'I *was* Rosalind Percival.'

Her companion's face lit with recognition. 'Of course! No wonder I knew we'd met! You've hardly changed.' She grinned at the ridiculous nature of the statement. 'A bit maybe. Little Combe? Late fifties, early sixties? Top class in the junior school? I was Juliet Cranfield then. You had an older brother, Simon. Very good-looking.'

'Four brothers. Simon's the youngest...But of course! How could I forget! Heavens, we sat next to each other for a whole year! We'd not long moved to the parish, but we were best friends. And didn't we both go on to Grammar School? You were there in the first year, anyway.

And then we lost touch. You moved away, didn't you?'

'Sort of. I went off to boarding school: Cheltenham.'

'Of course! We wrote to each other for a bit didn't we?'

'Yes, I believe we may have done.' Something in her manner suggested to Rosalind that the memory made her feel uncomfortable in some way, though if so she recovered quickly enough and went on, 'I've often wondered what became of you. Once or twice I thought of trying *Friends Reunited*, but couldn't quite pluck up the courage.'

'I'm a complete novice where things like that are concerned, so I guess it wouldn't have worked. But how astonishing! What brings you here? And where are you living now?'

A shadow crossed Juliet's face and then disappeared as quickly as it had come. 'We've bought that old house near the river, three miles out of Meadhope. Holywell?'

'So you are the 'people from London'—news gets around, you see! I heard it had been sold at last. It's been empty since I came here—it seemed such a shame. You must have a lot to do to it?'

'Oh, you can't begin to imagine! It's a ruin!

But Leo—my husband—he's keen to get going. It's his dream to do up an old place. And I'll do the interior design. That's my field. It'll take years though.'

Someone was at Rosalind's elbow, anxious to get her attention; the dark, unassuming figure of churchwarden Keith Grey. 'Look, I've got to go now—but you must come round some time, for a coffee perhaps.' She grinned suddenly. 'Or shall I put you down for a pastoral visit? I had actually intended to call, once you'd had time to settle in.'

'So long as you don't talk religion. Not my thing, but I'm badly in need of a good gossip. We've so much catching up to do!' Juliet began to scrabble in her bag, bringing out pen and paper. 'Here, I'll give you my mobile number, then you can check I'll be in. Not that I'm likely to be out much, but you never know.'

Rosalind slipped the paper in her pocket and then gave her attention to her churchwarden.

Much later, when the stalls had been cleared —unsold items boxed up for the village charity shop or the next sale, money counted and handed over to the treasurer, chairs and tables stacked away, floor swept and the doors locked —Rosalind, briefly looking into her study before putting her feet up for what remained of the day, took the paper from her pocket and resolved to make that visit to Juliet as soon as possible. She would enjoy picking up the threads of an old friendship, but she sensed too that there was some deep trouble, untouched upon today. Perhaps Juliet needed a friend rather more than she did.

Then she smiled to herself. Who was she kidding? A friend was *exactly* what she needed, a real ordinary down-to-earth woman friend. Alastair was her best friend, her companion and confidant in everything. But there were times when she longed to have a woman's company. As rector she felt she could not single out any one of her parishioners over another, so her only close friends lived far away. But Holywell was right on the fringe of her parish, set apart. She could enjoy a friendship with someone living there without hurting or offending anyone else, without her other parishioners even knowing about it. And Juliet had been such a good friend, once. Would they be able, as adults, to revive that old childhood closeness?

Later that day, Juliet chipped away at the plaster in the room that would, they hoped, eventually become their dining room. It came loose only too easily, damp and cracked as it was. Leo, accepting reluctantly that making their everyday reception rooms habitable ought to have a higher priority than exhuming some interesting but otherwise impractical hidden feature, was working on the opposite wall, but had little to say, beyond an occasional comment on what he found or a suggestion as to what could be done about it. They felt no particular need to talk. Once, they would have shared the companionable silence of two people who know each other too well to need mere words. Now, it was rather a case of being aware of emotions it would be dangerous to touch on or bring into the open, for fear that it would destroy the last threads that held them together. It was a long time since there had been any real sense of intimacy between them. Moving here had not altered that at all, had only given them something safe to talk about from time to time. Any conversation they had nowadays merely skimmed the surface of their lives, absorbed by the trivial, ignoring everything that was important. But at least it gave them an illusion of companionship, the means of living together with some degree of civility.

As the fragments of plaster fell about her, covering her old trainers with a grey dust, Juliet went over in her mind all that had happened today, the meeting with Rosalind in particular. A part of her rejoiced that she had rediscovered a friend. It had been such a sudden impulse, to go into the church hall. If it had not been for the coincidence of seeing Luke's name, she would probably not have done so. It seemed almost as if Luke himself had taken a hand in things, had brought the two of them together again. It came back to her now how close they had been, she and Rosalind—Rosie, complete in her memory, fiery hair, green eyes; laughing, whispering, inseparable, sharing secrets, jokes, all the things girls of that age loved to share with their best friends—though not perhaps the sort of things girls nowadays, far more worldly-wise, would find interesting. It had been more Enid Blyton-type secret societies than boys and make-up.

They had been glad to pass for the Grammar School together—and grief-stricken when her parents had decided to send her to Cheltenham Ladies College. They would always be friends, they had sworn. Nothing should ever be allowed to come between them. But it had, and the thought of it now made Juliet feel ashamed, even after all this time. She had loved her new school, quickly made friends, and on her return to Little Combe during the school holidays had laid claim as of right to a whole new range of interests, a whole new circle, in which there was no place for Rosalind. The vicarage children had no horses and did not ride, Rosalind wore shabby second-hand clothes, she even had traces of a local accent, which was something Juliet had quickly lost. In fact, in common with her new friends, Juliet had come to look down on the old one, almost without knowing she was doing it. Did Rosalind remember anything of this? Had she even noticed? She felt just a little uncomfortable at the thought of the coming meeting, which Rosalind had phoned to arrange for the following Tuesday. Of all her friends, Rosalind was the one to whom, once, she had felt closest. Could they revive that now, when she so badly needed a friend? Did she even want to risk launching into another friendship, after being let down so badly by the old ones?

With one wall cleared of plaster and another three quarters done, they stopped for a hasty supper, and then went to bed. One thing about all this house renovation, Juliet reflected: it made one physically tired and ready for sleep, a healthy tiredness quite unlike the debilitating weariness of bereavement. She pulled the curtains against the night—it was windy, with sudden sharp showers of rain—and snuggled under the duvet, falling quickly asleep.

She had not been sleeping for very long when she was jolted into wakefulness. She often woke like this, after the first deep sleep, to be tormented by memories, by grief. But she knew this was different. This time something external had disturbed her. What was it? The wind?

The branches of the ancient apple trees were creaking and groaning in the darkness beyond the window, yet for some reason Juliet was quite sure that this was not what had woken her.

And she was afraid. She kept her eyes closed, in case on opening them she should see something to give her real cause for fear. Yet what could there be?

Steps—that was what she'd heard, and there they were again: footsteps on ancient boards, setting them creaking rhythmically, purposefully. This was nothing like the random intermittent sounds of an old house settling for the night.

'Leo?' Her voice emerged as a faint squeak. Even if it was Leo out there (and surely it must be?), he could not have heard her. *You're being stupid!* she told herself. *It'll just be him, going to the loo. Perfectly normal, something he does at some point every night. What on earth is scary about that?*

She tried to persuade herself to get up and open the bedroom door, just for reassurance. But what if there was nothing there, what then? And why did her thoughts keep straying to that doorway, the ancient arch, the bricks that filled it?

She switched the bedside lamp on, its gentle light illuminating the room, which looked exactly as it always did. The sound had ceased now. Nothing to be afraid of. She was just being silly. She'd probably had a nightmare, now forgotten, and woken herself from it; hence the feeling of terror.

But she left the light on while she drifted into sleep and did not turn it off until she woke to the grey dawn.

Chapter Three

Holywell was a beautiful house, there was no doubt about that. Rosalind halted on the stony approach road and gazed at it lying bathed in all the sunlight of the October morning. She'd walked past it once, early in her ministry here, when she'd been trying to explore a different footpath in the parish on each of her days off, but had never been inside. All she knew was that it had been empty since the death of the old farmer who had worked its land for more than sixty years. The farm had been sold, the land absorbed into a neighbouring farm, but no one had moved into the farmhouse—until now. Presumably the fact that it was a listed building and would cost a fortune to restore and maintain had put off potential buyers.

Rosalind saw a charming hotchpotch of buildings in the soft local sandstone, at one end an ancient tower giving way to more domestic architecture, as if each century until the eighteenth had left its mark, at which point it had declined from a manor house to a simple farmhouse and its subsequent owners had simply made do and adapted what was left. Roofed with great stone slabs patterned with moss and lichen, a material reflected in the paved yard behind the house, it looked as natural there as any of the trees that sheltered it, as if it had grown from the slope of the hill behind the byres that edged the further side of the yard.

She leant her bike against the wall beside the small red Subaru (brand new, she noted), and made her way towards the solid oak door that appeared to be the main entrance to the house. Juliet must have been watching for her arrival, for the door opened as she reached it.

'Rosie! Come on in!' They kissed, polite air kisses. 'Have you cycled all the way here? You must be exhausted.'

'I'm trying to do my bit for the environment. There aren't that many times I can manage without the car. Good for the figure though.' Rosalind laughed: 'My son says we should get a pony and trap.'

'That would be fun. We've got stables going free if you decide to go in for it.' She gestured towards the outbuildings.

Something stirred in Rosalind's mind. 'Won't you be keeping horses yourself? You used to ride, didn't you?'

'I'd love to take it up again, but it's so long… We shall see.' Juliet led the way into a flagged passage that soon opened into the vast farmhouse kitchen.

'What a wonderful room!' Rosalind exclaimed. 'And it looks properly lived in. You must have done a lot of work already.'

'We had the whole place rewired before we moved in, and some plumbing and one or two other essentials. But there's still masses to do. Though this room was probably the one that needed least work.'

'From what I heard, old Fred Peart had more or less lived in the one room for years before he died. It would have been this one, I imagine.'

'He was the last person to live here, wasn't he?'

'He died not long before I arrived in the parish. Ninety years old and still farming right to the end. I'm told he farmed as if he'd go on for ever, though he had no one to leave it all to. The last of his line...' Rosalind moved towards the far windows and looked out over the garden and the green valley beyond. 'It's amazing how light it all is, for an old building—it's south facing isn't it? Do you have much land with it?'

'As far as the wall there, just beyond the apple trees. Enough for the Good Life if we decide that's what we want, chickens or whatever.'

'Have you got grandchildren to come and enjoy it with you?'

A tiny pause, then Juliet heard herself say: 'No family. Just ourselves, just the two of us.' And immediately thought, *Why did I do that? Why did I deny Luke, as if he'd never existed?* She scoured her mind for something else to say, to cover her embarrassment and what she felt was the awkward silence that had followed it, but in the end it was Rosalind who spoke first.

'What period is this part of the house?'

'Mostly eighteenth century, I think. There were so many documents with the deeds that we haven't had time yet to look through them all, though I'm not sure how much information there is in them. It took our solicitors for ever to sort them all out; we thought we'd never get moved. Believe it or not, we first saw the house way back in April! What we do hope to do, eventually, is get an expert in to look it over and tell us which bit of it was built when. We're due a visit from English Heritage soon—they may be able to point us in the right direction.' She moved towards the Aga. 'Coffee first, or a guided tour?'

'Oh, coffee please! Then we can catch up a bit.'

Juliet busied herself with kettle and cafetière,

set biscuits on the scrubbed oak table. 'Hope you don't mind slumming it in the kitchen. It's the warmest place in the house. The Aga's taken some getting used to, but I thank God for it daily. You'd never believe how cold this house is, even when it's sunny outside.'

'Cool on hot days I suppose.' Rosalind took a seat on one of the rush-bottomed kitchen chairs.

'Do you ever get hot days in Meadhope?' Juliet grinned. 'Silly question—it's lovely today, and has been since we moved in.'

'St Luke's little summer,' said Rosalind.

Juliet darted a glance at her. 'What's that?'

'St Luke's tide—his feast day was last Thursday, the 18th, which is why we have our fair around now. He's our patronal saint. There's often a spell of fine weather around now, so it's St Luke's little summer.'

'Oh!' *St Luke*—they had moved here in St Luke's tide! So many things were happening that seemed somehow more than just coincidence…She sat down rather suddenly opposite her guest and tried to be matter-of-fact. 'We've the house to ourselves. Leo's spending the day at the tip.' She grinned. 'He's clearing out the rubbish that was left in one of the barns —byres, I think you call them round here. Rusty old farm machinery, not even fit for a museum.'

'What does he do? Apart from restoring the house, of course. I imagine that's a pretty full-time occupation.'

'He's an accountant. Or was. Retired from the City. He may do a bit of consultancy work now and then, just to keep his hand in.'

'And you? You said interior design was your thing?'

'I had quite a thriving little business in Chelsea.'

'You must miss it.'

'Not really. Nothing to keep us there.' Nothing, except painful memories; not even any friends, since they had so let her down. All the things that, before Luke's death, had seemed important to her—her work, her personal trainer with regular sessions at the gym, her round of meetings with friends for coffee or lunch—had all crumbled away afterwards, seeming at best irrelevant, at worst utterly unhelpful.

'It's a huge step, moving so far from everything familiar. Has it been a big culture shock?'

'Not so far. In any case, I suppose I'm a country girl at heart. Little Combe was hardly a metropolis. Do you ever go back there?'

'I did once, when we passed that way on holiday. It had changed such a lot—all prettied up, full of wealthy weekenders instead of the feudal set-up of farm workers and landowners I remembered. What about you? Are your parents still alive?'

'No. My mother drank herself to death— well, you may remember how she was; always liked a drink. I suppose she was bored a lot of the time. My father wasn't the most exciting of husbands—such a workaholic!' Her father, Rosalind recalled, had been a hospital consultant of some kind. 'Anyway, he didn't last long after she died. And what with going away to school, I didn't have many friends in the place anyway.' She paused a moment. 'I'm just trying to think who I remember whom you might have known. Patricia somebody, Pat— Ashley, that was it!'

'Oh yes! She was the one who was so awful to poor Miss Tregoning—do you remember Miss Tregoning?'

'Who could forget her? That hairstyle! Such a strange colour! I think she fancied herself as some sort of Hollywood starlet manquée. I liked her though. She had a good heart. But Pat Ashley—she wasn't kind, really rather cruel, but then little girls are, aren't they?' *Not just the notorious Pat either,* Juliet thought with a stir of unease, which she quickly banished. 'Do you remember the plastic spider?'

'Oh I do! It looked so real. And Miss Tregoning hated spiders! She was terrified.'

'Jumped up on her chair! And then went bright red when she realised, and lost her balance. Oh, poor soul!' She giggled. 'Don't we sound just like Enid Blyton's Malory Towers' girls? It was all so innocent, wasn't it?'

They reminisced and laughed and gossiped and time passed more quickly for Juliet than it had for as long as she could remember. Perhaps that was why she had denied Luke's existence, so that she should somehow have this little interlude of trivial enjoyment, without pain. There was relief in it, though as she came out of it she was conscious too of a sense of guilt that had nothing to do with regret for an ancient friendship broken off. For just that short space of time she had not thought of Luke at all. She could not recall when that had last happened to her—never, she thought, since that April day. How could she—? Yet it had been good, refreshment for her spirit.

'I think it's time for the tour of the house!' she declared, as the talk faltered into a lengthy if companionable silence. So many memories!

'I'd love to—though I mustn't be too long. I've a round of visits to make this afternoon.'

'I can't imagine being a vicar.' Juliet paused by the door leading out of the kitchen at its further side. 'Especially as a woman. Have you found it hard? Have you had any trouble from the anti-women-priest brigade?'

'Oh, there are always people who oppose the ordination of women in principle, even now, probably always will be, but most people accept me completely—take me for granted even. I'm just like any other Anglican priest—they like me or they don't, they compare me with vicar so-and-so who ruled this parish for thirty years back in the sixties, to my detriment usually. But then that's true of any parish. Being a country priest is much more the traditional role than it is in the town. I rather like that.'

Juliet led the way out of the kitchen through another room—empty, chill, with peeling plaster, some of which had been stripped from the walls ('One day this will be our dining room') which opened into a further wide, low-ceilinged room, with windows the length of the garden side of the house and a large stone fireplace. It was partly furnished with two large sofas and a couple of armchairs, covered with dustsheets. 'This will be our drawing room, eventually. And here—' leading Rosalind out into a passage running the width of the house, 'the door here opens into the garden. We think there was another door at the other end, but it's been blocked up, maybe to keep the house warmer.' She crossed the passage to the great studded oak door that faced them. 'This is the oldest part of the house we think, the tower.' She pushed the door open against her sudden sense of reluctance.

Rosalind gazed around in awe. 'This is amazing! A real baronial hall!'

'And as you see, holes in the roof, woodworm in the beams—though we've had them treated. Damp and cold. But with massive potential. We're not quite sure what for, but it certainly has potential.' She gestured across the room, trying to sound matter-of-fact. 'See that blocked up doorway there? Leo thinks there's a spiral stair beyond it that once led to some upstairs rooms that have been demolished. You can see high up—there! You can see there must have been another floor.'

'Are you going to open it up?'

'Leo wants to.' Hastily trying to move away from the subject, Juliet led the way back, closing the door behind her with a sense of relief. 'Upstairs now—we have to go back through the kitchen.'

'How on earth do you find your way about?' Rosalind asked as they mounted the wide graceful staircase.

'With difficulty! Though we did at least have a floor plan from the estate agent, which has been invaluable. I'm just beginning to work it all out.'

Rosalind paused on the landing, gazing out of the long window that lit it. 'What a lovely view!'

'Do you know anything of the house's history? The agent said it went back to the twelfth century, but that might have been agent's speak.'

'If you want to find out more, try asking Keith Grey in the village. One of our churchwardens; Mill House, off the Black Fell road. He's done a lot of local research. Or there's Philippa Lee. In fact, Meadhope is awash with amateur local historians. There's sure to be someone knows something about the house, even though it isn't quite in the village.' She followed Juliet across the landing to the master bedroom. 'As you say, it's got huge potential, I can see that.'

'That's what attracted us. A good project for our retirement, with a lovely house at the end of it. It's ridiculous isn't it—this house cost a third of what we got for our flat in Chelsea, though we've exchanged three bedrooms for a potential six. The London housing market is mad.' She opened yet another door. 'This is my place— well, it will be when it's sorted properly. I guess it'll be last on the list.' She saw Rosalind take in the inevitable packing cases, still as the removers' had left them; the oak table, the small belongings ranged on it: organiser, sketchpads, pens and pencils, and a couple of photos of Luke: at two years old, and on holiday with his parents in Italy, standing beside Lake Como, grinning away, a mischievous fourteen-year-old, tanned and slender.

'A bonny baby,' Rosalind commented, 'and a good looking boy. They must be related. Or are they one and the same?'

Juliet was almost tempted to brush the question aside and change the subject. But something about the way Rosalind stood quietly there, just waiting, drew the truth from her. 'Luke. Our son.' Then in a rush because there was no other bearable way to do it: 'He was killed. A car crash. Just over a year ago. April the 16th. Easter time.'

'Oh Juliet, I'm so sorry!' Rosalind stood very still, her eyes in her friend's face. 'There aren't any words—'

'No.' That was a relief. She had heard so many of the wrong words, the clumsily inept phrases that only made the pain worse. 'Though aren't you supposed to find them?'

'I have children myself. I can't begin to imagine what it would be like to lose one of them. I don't even want to try.'

Juliet came over to the window and leaned with her back against the windowsill, so that the light was full on Rosalind's face as she turned towards her, but her own was in shadow.

'It would turn your lives upside down,' Rosalind added gently.

'I remember everything about it, when the news came. From the moment I opened the door and saw the police, I knew, straightaway, before they said anything. It was in their faces. They were as kind as they could be, but that didn't make it any better. They phoned Leo for me—he was at a conference. Not that I wanted him there—' She was conscious of Rosalind's silence, the unasked question. 'He'd insisted on giving Luke that car, a fast sports car, a reward for passing his driving test. It was a stupid thing to do. I begged him not to—we had a row about it, but he wouldn't listen. You know how many young men have accidents, driving too fast.

What do you expect any boy to do behind the wheel of a sporty Mazda? They said he hadn't been drinking, but then he didn't need to. The speed would go straight to his head.' Her voice had grown harsh with emotion, the words suddenly rasped into silence.

'Your poor husband! He must have felt so dreadful afterwards, so guilty…'

'I suppose…I don't know. He's never said so, not in so many words.' Did he feel guilty? She had no idea. That he missed Luke and mourned him, that was obvious enough, or had been, though he never said much about his feelings and she doubted if they were as scorchingly painful as hers. But guilty? He ought to feel it, if there was any justice. It ought to be gnawing away at him beyond endurance, so that he could scarcely bear to go on living.

'And you can't forgive him?'

'No.' She gave a rueful half-smile that was without warmth or softness. 'You're wondering why I stay with him. I wonder too, except there's no one else. I did come close to leaving him, but then—I suppose I'm afraid to be alone. And he's the only one who knew Luke as I did. Luke was very like him. That makes me angry sometimes.'

'So you came here to escape?'

'To start again. That was the idea anyway. I'm still not convinced it was a good idea, or that it'll work.'

'You've left all your friends behind, everyone you knew.'

'My friends cut themselves off. Not one of them was really there for me when it happened. You know what one of them said, my so-called best friend, the one I thought would stand by me through everything? *'I know how you feel'*— that was the first thing. It's outrageous! How could she possibly know? She hadn't even any children herself. And then, as if that wasn't bad enough, she said, *'How sad that you didn't have other children.'* As if that would have made it any easier! Luke was Luke, not someone else. If we'd had six children it would have been the same.' Rosalind murmured her agreement, gently, without words. 'Anyway, they dropped me, some of them straight away—I saw one even cross the road when she saw me coming. Others—well, I didn't fit their stereotype of the grieving mother, I suppose. I was so angry, furiously angry, not just with Leo, but everyone, everything. On the surface anyway. It's easier to be angry than—well! The only one who understood, at all, was Luke's girlfriend Katie, though God knows she had every reason to cut us out of her life. She was in the car that night, though she doesn't remember anything about the accident. She got out alive, but she was very badly injured. She spent months in hospital afterwards. But she's been great, kept in touch and likes to talk about Luke. There's been no one else for her since then.'

A pause, then: 'Are you still angry?'

'Not enough. I wish I was. Now—it's kind of empty. Sometimes I just feel so tired. I want—' She fell silent, the tears suddenly very close to the surface. Then she went on in a whisper, 'That's just it—I don't really know what I do want. I would just like to have something to aim for, to live for— Moving here was supposed to do that, but…I don't know.'

Rosalind's arms were about her shoulders, just holding her, without words. She allowed herself to accept a measure of comfort, to rest on the sense of being enclosed by an offered support that asked absolutely nothing in return.

Or did it? Rosalind was not, of course, simply a friend rediscovered. Recalling that fact, Juliet drew back suddenly, 'I don't believe in God, you know!' she said sharply.

'That's OK.'

'I didn't before all this, not really. But now— I never could now, never!' She glared at

Rosalind. 'I suppose you're going to say God loves me, aren't you? Funny way of showing it then!'

'I believe He does. But I imagine it doesn't feel like it to you.' She gazed at Juliet, who sensed that Rosalind was aware of the tangle of anger and pain that tormented her, and was trying to know how best to help. Somehow she seemed to understand that doing and saying nothing, just simply being there, a willing listener, a friend, even a buffer for the pain and anger, was the only kind of consolation that could be acceptable. This was friendship, as it should be.

Juliet detached herself and stood gazing out of the window, Rosalind at her side. 'I'm sorry. I don't usually lose it like that.'

'Do you talk to Leo about the way you feel?'

'God no! We don't talk—or only about practical things, how we're going to do the bathroom, what colour to paint the dining room, that sort of stuff. Ironic really: before all this I'd have said we had a good marriage. Right from the start, when we met—a friend's party it was—there was that connection, an instant connection. But not any more.'

'Does he know that you blame him for what happened?'

'I guess he knows.'

'You haven't told him?'

'How can I? What do I say: that I think he's a murderer, or little better than? It would destroy our marriage.'

'But that's what you think, and it's festering away inside you. Isn't that already undermining your marriage?'

'I have to admit I sometimes wonder if what we've got is still a marriage in any real sense. Or are we just two people living together, from habit and for convenience?'

'Yet you're together still, in spite of everything.' Rosalind paused a moment, then said, 'There's one thing I've learned, one way and another. It takes a very long time to adjust to losing someone.'

'Do you ever 'adjust' to losing your child?'

'Adjust, maybe, in the sense of learning to go on living. But getting over it? No, of course not.'

'I want to laugh again.'

'You did today.'

'So I did!' She smiled. 'Thank you for that. And thank you for listening. I haven't asked you a thing about yourself.'

'There's not much to tell really. And I'm afraid it'll have to wait. I really must go now.'

'You won't stay for a bite of lunch?'

'I'd love to, but I need to look in at home before the afternoon visits. I have a son with problems, you see.' She said it gently, as if aware that she was privileged; her son, however damaged, was still living. 'But we'll get together again soon—if that's what you'd like. How about Monday week, November 5th, lunch in Durham somewhere? Monday's my day off, and I usually get out of the house and away from the phone for the day—though not next Monday, unfortunately.'

'I'd like that!'

They agreed a place and time, then Rosalind said, 'And you know where I am if you want to let off steam a bit before then.'

'I can't offer much in return.'

'Don't you believe it! I could let off steam for England about my mother-in-law. Bore you to tears!'

As Rosalind cycled away from Holywell, her mobile rang. She pedalled to the side of the road and answered it, hearing her mother-in-law's precise Edinburgh vowels with a sinking heart. 'Oh, Jessie—hello! What can I do?'

'I am in need of potatoes. I thought you might have telephoned this morning, to make sure I wanted for nothing.'

'I'm sorry, but I haven't been anywhere near the shops this morning.' Why did she still feel a twinge of guilt that she hadn't done something she had never intended to do, nor believed she ought to have done? Besides: 'Didn't Alastair get you potatoes on Saturday? I'm sure I remember seeing some.'

'They were Desirée.' She made it sound like some sort of disease. 'You know I like Maris Piper.'

'I'm sure he will have got them because that's all he could find. Have you tried them?'

'Of course I have tried them! Most unsatisfactory they were too. You can take the rest away when you bring me the Maris Pipers. I shall expect you this afternoon.' Before Rosalind could reply she had rung off. Rosalind made a very un-Christian exclamation under her breath and put the phone away. Then she took a few moments to breathe deeply and calm herself before cycling on.

They had talked last night, she and Alastair, about the problem of his mother and her ever more frequent demands on their time and attention. It was not for the first time, by any means. These demands, with her steadily increasing frailty, were becoming harder and harder to deal with. They had been through all this a few years ago, when it had become clear that Jessie could no longer manage alone in the vast house in her native Edinburgh suburb of Morningside, to which she had returned after the death of Alastair's father nearly thirty years before. It had taken an exhausting amount of time and effort to persuade her to move nearer to them, to a small easily-maintained modern house. Now it was becoming clear that another crisis was looming, that she did need far more help than she had in the past, not as a temporary stopgap, but as a permanent arrangement—at least until the next crisis brought another stage in her decline. The one certain thing was that life was not going to get any easier for Jessie nor, as a result, for her son and daughter-in-law. 'Do we broach the subject of a care package again?' Alastair had sounded weary at the very idea.

'If you think you can, it's worth a try.'

'You know what she'll say?'

'I do indeed: *I've got you two. Why do I need strangers coming into my home?*'

But today (after a snatched sandwich lunch in the rectory kitchen, for which Josh did not join her as she'd hoped) Rosalind slipped into the small village supermarket and bought a bag of Maris Piper potatoes, before setting out on her round of visits. At the end of the afternoon —before daily evensong and the need to think about supper—she looked in on her mother-in-law at her tidy modern house in a quiet close not far from the rectory. 'I've brought your potatoes,' she said cheerfully as she stepped through the back door. She had, as usual, braced herself before knocking and opening it, with a silent prayer, *Lord, give me patience!*

Jessie emerged from her lounge, walking slowly from door frame to hall stand to kitchen doorpost to the table beside Rosalind, who knew better than to offer her help within the house—outside, yes, Jessie was ready enough to accept a proffered arm, expected it indeed, but here she preferred the more reliable support of inanimate objects. She cast a suspicious glance at the bag Rosalind held, peering at the label with a 'Hmph!' of acceptance. 'You can put them in the rack. And take those others away. You will make use of them.'

Not ourselves having the taste and discernment to appreciate the perfection of a Maris Piper potato, reflected Rosalind with an inward smile, while she carried out Jessie's instructions. After that, there was a light bulb to be changed, a mattress to be turned and the bed to be made afterwards, and then Jessie suggested she tidy the understairs cupboard. 'Another time. I'm going to be late for evensong.'

'No one ever attends. You can afford to put your duty to your family first.'

Do I remind her that I'm supposed to put God first; that even if no one else is there, this half hour spent with God is an essential part of the day, along with the service of morning prayer that begins it? No, she wouldn't say it, because it would sound preachy and rude and Jessie would simply be offended. 'I'm sorry —I do have to go now.' She kissed her cheek. 'Much love. See you soon.'

As it happened there *was* someone else at evening prayer today—two people in fact, Sally Oldfield from Moor Farm and her six-year-old daughter Grace, on their way back from the village school. 'Just a chance to touch base, have a little time out,' Sally had explained on a previous occasion.

And then, a little later, back at the rectory, there was Alastair, a loving listening presence who saw at once that she was tired and offered to cook the evening meal, while she sat in comfort with a glass of wine and told him about her day. 'I'll sort out Mother's cupboard on Saturday,' he promised. 'And we'll have chips tomorrow, with her despised Desirée potatoes. I'll get some fish at lunch time. Fish and chips. How does that sound?'

'Perfect comfort food.' She kissed him. 'You're wonderful—Do you know that?'

'Of course,' he said. 'You are the envy of Meadhope!' Then: 'How was your visit to Holywell? Lots of girlie gossip?'

'Some, which was fun. But Juliet's had a lot of trouble. Still has really. They lost a son, you see, their only son. Just last year.'

'How terrible.' She could see him trying to imagine something so appalling happening to them; and then not wanting to. That reminded him too, as it did her, of a grief nearer to home. 'Is Josh joining us this evening?' Often their son would remain in his room all evening, or alternatively go out with no indication of where he was going or why. They only guessed that he didn't really bother to eat.

'He's been upstairs all day, as far as I know.' He'd eaten the sandwich she'd left him—or at least, it was no longer wrapped in clingfilm in the fridge—and there'd been a response of sorts when she'd called out to him on her return home this evening.

Alastair chopped an onion vigorously. 'What are we going to do about him?'

'I don't know. I really don't. There isn't much we can do if he doesn't want us to.' This was another conversation they often had, which

—like the one about Alastair's mother—went round and round in circles, fruitlessly. 'He seemed so much more himself when he got back from Sophie's.' He had lately returned from a visit to his sister and her growing family. Rosalind recalled another hopeful sign. 'Haven't you noticed—he's even started washing again? But it doesn't seem to be lasting, the improvement.'

'It could be that seeing Sophie so happy and settled simply reminded him of what he's missing, of what might have been.'

'Mm…As I was saying to Juliet this afternoon, it takes a very long time to adjust after you've lost someone. Stating the blindingly obvious I suppose. Oh Alastair, why is it that everything I say seems to come out as a cliché? When has anyone ever been consoled by a trite repetition of some hackneyed phrase?'

'Just because the words have been used before doesn't mean they're not heartfelt does it, or meaningful either? After all, every word we use has been around a very long time. It's the feeling behind them that matters.'

Rosalind recalled what Juliet had said about the friends who had betrayed her by saying the wrong thing. Very likely they had felt every bit as much sympathy and concern as Juliet could have asked for, but that had not been enough. 'If you're in real pain, with your feelings in a complete turmoil, I guess you don't care what the person speaking to you is feeling or what their intentions are. You haven't got room for understanding. If they get it wrong, it just makes things worse.'

Alastair turned towards her. 'Oh hold on now, Rosie, you'll convince yourself you're doomed to failure no matter what if you're not careful!' He reached over with the bottle of wine. 'Here, have a top-up and forget about other people's problems.'

'Even Josh's?'

'Even Josh's. For now at least. I guess time is what he needs and we can't make it go any faster. Shall I put garlic in this risotto? You haven't got a meeting this evening have you?'

Chapter Four

'Do you remember Juliet Cranfield?' asked Rosalind. 'From Little Combe. We were best friends.'

'Oh yes,' came her mother's voice over the line—they were keeping in touch with their usual weekly phone call. 'Yes, I remember her. Why?'

There was an odd touch of acidity in Anne Percival's voice, which startled Rosalind, though she did not immediately investigate it. 'She's turned up here, living just a mile or so away. It was wonderful to meet her again after all these years! Of all the people I've lost touch with, she was the one I minded about most. I don't think I've ever been closer to any of my friends as I was to her—though it was a very long time ago of course.'

'Is she still very horsey? In with the county set?'

Rosalind laughed. 'Mum, you sound positively disapproving! That's not like you.'

'Well, she was too high and mighty to come to your birthday party, once she was away at public school. Your thirteenth birthday—or was it your fourteenth? It hurt you a lot at the time.'

Rosalind strained to remember any such incident. 'You know, if that happened I've quite forgotten. All I remember was that she went away just after we went on to Grammar school. We swore to be friends for ever, but somehow lost touch. I didn't even remember that she still lived in the village.'

'Self-protection perhaps. You *were* very hurt.'

Rosalind laughed. 'Well, I obviously don't bear grudges if I've forgotten the whole thing! Or maybe I've just got a very bad memory. Anyway, she's not in the county set any longer, as far as I can tell. She's been living in London and lost a son, just last year. If I'd known there was anything to hold against her, I couldn't have done, not in the face of all that.'

'No—no, you couldn't. Of course not.' There was a little silence, then her mother said, 'I did like her, before all that blew up. She was a bright little thing, the nearest you got to a sister, with all those brothers. I suppose that's why it seemed so bad when she let you down like that.'

'Ah well, water under the bridge. That's enough about me. How are you then?' Anne Percival lived in Hampshire, close to Rosalind's elder brother Jack.

'I'm fine. I've got Hannah staying with me at the moment.' Hannah was Jack's youngest.

'Is she between jobs again then? Oh dear!'

'Well, you know Hannah. She's good company though. I'm hoping she'll find something near here.'

'Finger's crossed!' Not for the first time, Rosalind felt a pang of regret that she did not live nearer to her mother and brothers. If nothing else, it would have been so much easier to care for her own mother in her old age than it was to look after Jessie Maclaren. Anne Percival was still fit and well and enjoying an active social life, but even if she hadn't been, the basis of their relationship was a deep love and trust that could surely have withstood any difficulty.

Mustn't think like that! Rosalind rebuked herself. Being near her mother would not make her any less responsible for caring for Jessie, so that was that. 'Have you any plans for Christmas? You're very welcome to come to us.'

'I think it's Richard's turn this year. He's been very insistent. I have to keep you all happy you know.'

'You do, Mum—you do!'

The following morning, as she drove to her other church in the hamlet of Ashburn for the midweek communion service, she pondered what her mother had told her. It was odd that she had no recollection of Juliet's rejection of her, not even as a sense of reserve about her former friend. She had felt only an unconditional delight at their meeting. There was something to be said for having a bad memory. She offered up a little prayer of thanksgiving for friendship before concentrating on parking the car at the side of the road near the church.

Inside St John's church, Daphne Wynyard was optimistically setting out service books on the table by the door. 'Do you know something I don't?' Rosalind grinned, glancing at the neat row.

'Must be prepared. In case.'

'Is Jeremy likely to be with us?'

Jeremy was Daphne's adult son, still living at home and ostensibly the man of the house, which he had inherited at his father's death, though no one had any illusions as to who ruled at Ashburn Hall. 'Not today. To be honest, Rosalind, I don't know what's got into him. Fiftieth birthday next week—big party and so forth, all planned for months. And now instead of giving a hand with the preparations he's taken himself off to stay with friends in the Midlands. Left it all to me.' She raised her eyes heavenwards. 'Men!' She finished arranging the service books and straightened. 'Still, Caroline and Humphrey arrive tomorrow, so I shan't be without assistance.' Caroline was her daughter. 'You will be joining us, won't you?' Rosalind and Alastair had received their invitation some time ago, though neither of them could be regarded as particular friends of Jeremy Wynyard.

'Of course,' said Rosalind, not admitting how desperately they'd both tried to find a valid excuse to refuse the invitation.

Behind her, the church door opened and an old lady hobbled in, stick tapping on the stone flags. 'Ah, Irene, good to see you!' Then, allowing Rosalind no opportunity to speak to the newcomer, Daphne went on, 'Rosalind, while I think of it—you might want to include this in your prayers: the Halls are selling up.'

'Oh dear! That's a blow! It's one after another at the moment isn't it?'

'Well, I guess foot and mouth coming back this year was the last straw. I know it didn't get to us here, but after the last time—! Then what with this awful summer, and milk prices so low —well, who in his right mind would be in farming? Especially dairy farming like Derek Hall.'

'I know—I know.'

'Been there for generations. God knows who'll buy the place.'

By now, three others had gathered in the church—all elderly ladies—and Rosalind managed to extricate herself from listening to Daphne and make her way to the vestry to robe for the service. Going to Ashburn always took her back to the days at Little Combe and the apparently changeless feudal society that her father had served. Though by now even that had changed, more perhaps than Ashburn ever would.

Afterwards, the small congregation had coffee together at the back of the church, where a tray stood with kettle and cups and a jar of instant coffee. 'Filthy stuff, I know,' Daphne said, 'but not as bad as that fair trade muck you have at Meadhope.' She caught Rosalind's expression and went on, 'I have a great respect for you, Rosalind. You have a greater understanding of country life than I gave you credit for when you first came on the scene. But all this fair trade business—too much the sandals and beard brigade for my taste!'

'I don't think I'm growing a beard just yet,' Rosalind retorted with a grin, which Daphne returned cheerfully.

'You know what I mean. All this lefty stuff.

Global warming, fair trade—You know it doesn't really do any good, don't you?'

This was a subject Rosalind had discussed before, both with Daphne personally and with Ashburn's Parochial Church Council, and always fruitlessly, in spite of the fact that she had carefully looked into Daphne's arguments and assembled more than enough material to demolish them wholesale. Daphne was impervious to any argument she did not instinctively support; empirical evidence made no difference whatsoever. Today Rosalind did not even try to argue the point, beyond saying mildly, 'Well, you know what I think about that, Daphne. Maybe we can have another talk before the next PCC.'

She drove home, smiling to herself with rueful recognition of her helplessness against the force of nature that was Daphne Wynyard. No wonder Jeremy escaped from home when he could!

As Rosalind stepped into the rectory, Josh was coming downstairs. His hair—flame coloured, like hers—was tangled, and he'd clearly not shaved this morning. Her heart sank.

'I thought you were going to help with the packing today?' Durham Diocese had a link with the diocese of Lesotho in southern Africa, and—among other things—regularly despatched much-needed items, donated by well-wishers, to the link representatives in the country. Since Josh had spent his time working for VSO in Lesotho, he had lately begun, now and then, to help out with the link, which his parents had seen as a hopeful sign.

'Didn't feel like it. I'm not convinced it does any good.'

'Bad day?'

'Bad night.' He looked at her with an apology in his eyes—which she saw were brimming with tears again. She hugged him.

'Come and have some lunch. I made some soup yesterday.'

He gave a shaky laugh. 'You and your soup, Mum! If the world boils away to nothing you'll still be offering soup as a cure for all ills.'

'Well, it's not just the eating of it, it's the making too. Very soothing in moments of stress, I've always found.'

They sat together in the kitchen, with the soup steaming gently before them. 'Miriam was a great believer in comfort food too,' he said. 'You'd have got on well.'

'I'm sure we should. It's good when you talk about her—I almost feel we really did meet and get to know one another.'

He needed very little prompting to talk of her, so he did so now, until his mother had to leave for a meeting with the Area Dean. 'I'll go for a walk, I think,' he said. Then he kissed her. 'Thanks Mum.'

'What was that for?'

'Oh—you know!'

Which she did, really.

Josh set out walking briskly up the steep hill out of the village in the direction of the hilltop village of Black Fell. Part way up a car stopped beside him, the driver winding down the nearside window. 'Can I offer you a lift?'

The voice broke into his reverie and startled him. 'Oh—Sally! Hi! No, thanks very much, I'm out for the exercise.'

'You going on all right?' Sally Oldfield knew something of Josh's situation, as did most of his mother's parishioners. In some ways that made life easier, because people were less likely to blunder into his hurt places without realising what they were doing; in other ways, it made it harder, because so often they felt they needed to mention it in some way. But he liked Sally and they shared a mutual enthusiasm for computers that had brought them together on previous occasions.

'Yes thanks. How's business?'

After the foot and mouth outbreak six years before, Sally and her husband, having lost all their stock, had set up a business advising local farmers on any technological issues. They still farmed organically in a small way, but it was the computer business that fed them and their little daughter. 'Very good. More than we can cope with. You don't fancy a job with us I suppose?'

'Not at present, but thank you. I haven't decided what I want to do yet. But I'll bear it in mind.'

He watched her drive away, reflecting that she too had known troubles of her own. Six years ago, he had been a callow youth, self-obsessed as any other student, but he still recalled the year of foot and mouth with a shudder. He had seen how the brutal slaughter of their lovingly reared animals had shattered the Oldfields.

His sister too had suffered, as a young trainee vet caught up in the wholesale destruction of animals, instead of healing them in the way she had expected and so much wanted to do. He thought of Sophie now as he strode on up the hill. So much had changed in the years since then; she now had a husband

and family, living in happy domesticity with what seemed a perfect work-life balance, putting in occasional days at her husband's practice, enjoying her children, the circle of friendship with other young mothers in the area, a way of life that anyone might envy. And especially her brother, who had not even been able to snatch at the hope of such unalloyed happiness before the little he had was taken from him. Here he was, living at home as he had years ago, without an aim or a purpose. All he had left from the long years was the pain of loss.

At the top of the hill he paused and turned to look back the way he had come, over the valley and the far hills in the soft autumn light. It was beautiful, this valley that was now his home, but it did not feel like home and its beauty could not reach him. For him the most beautiful place still was that village in Africa, and above all the simplicity of the small round hut in which he and Miriam had spent their last days, high in the mountains, where the air was clear and pure and the sound of singing children reached them from the little school, and it had felt as if there must be healing lying in wait for them. Only that had been just a feeling, a delusion. There had been no healing, just this, the emptiness of life without her, of a future without hope.

He knew he should pull himself together, find something to do, something purposeful and satisfying. If nothing else, he knew how Miriam would regard his present aimless existence. She'd had no patience with self-pity. No one could be as lacking in self-centredness, in self-obsession, as Miriam. He would have been ashamed to face her as he was now because she would have despised him for it. Why then could he not break free of the terrible inertia of grief? He had hoped that by doing the little he could from here to help her countrymen and women, he would find some meaning again, but it had not worked. It had all seemed so pointless, such a drop in the ocean of need that he knew existed there, even perhaps a bit patronising, paternalistic.

Now, he shrugged, tried to move with purpose and determination, striding back down the hill. *Like the Grand Old Duke of York,* he thought wryly; *and about as useless.*

Juliet returned from her trip to the supermarket with the car full of provisions. She'd hoped by now to be ordering her groceries on line, but Holywell's broadband connection wasn't yet working, so she'd had to drive fourteen miles or so to the nearest quality supermarket. She wasn't sure where she was going to put everything once she got it into the house. She hadn't really intended to buy so much, but it was so good to be in a large store with an abundance of choice that it had all rather gone to her head. She parked in the yard —and saw with a surge of alarm that the Range Rover wasn't there. Leo had gone out.

She remembered those other times during the two years since Luke's death: saying nothing, giving no clue, he had simply gone, driven away, disappearing for days, sometimes weeks, while anxiety and panic had gnawed at her. Calls to his mobile had been met only with voicemail, those to his office the same, though she could never bring herself to leave a message. What if he never came back? she'd asked herself. What if he'd killed himself? For all that he enraged her, for all that sometimes she could hardly bear to be in the same room with him, she was still terrified of losing him, of being left truly alone. He always had returned eventually, silent, grim-faced, refusing to talk about it, but at least he had been there. Until the next time.

It had happened often in the months immediately following Luke's death, but then less often, and not at all since they'd made the decision to come here. She'd thought it was over, whatever it was. But now—

There was probably some simple explanation for his absence today; there had to be. Only, usually he told her if he was going out. Her hands were shaking as she unlocked the door.

Struggling into the house with the first batch of shopping, she was relieved to be swept by a conviction that she was not alone in the house. When she thought about it, the absence of the car did not necessarily mean Leo was not at home. Perhaps he'd taken the vehicle to the garage for service or repair, then got a lift back; it must be about due for a service. He hadn't said anything about it to her, but that meant nothing. It would be a relief to find that was the case, because it was a simple, normal, everyday thing.

'Leo!' she called. She put down her bags and went to the foot of the stairs, calling again. Her voice echoed in the silence, but the certainty remained that Leo was somewhere about.

Maybe he was working in the older part of the building, on the newly-discovered doorway. A little reluctantly, she went through the empty rooms just as far as the door that led into the hall. It stood very slightly open, but she made no attempt to push it wider. 'Leo!' she called. Then again: 'Leo!'

Nothing. Then there *was* something—a sound that she knew in her bones was not made by Leo. Every wild, illogical instinct warned her to turn and run, yet against her will she was drawn on, opening the door, walking through into the hall. It was empty—and yet not empty.

Her legs seemed directed by an impulse beyond herself, moving on across the room to where Leo had cleared the last of the plaster from the bricks and rubble that blocked up the old doorway, revealing its shape in full, the finely carved stonework that framed it. There she came to a halt, listening. What she heard was like the sound that had disturbed her sleep the other night, a steady rhythmic creaking, as if someone were pacing ancient boards overhead, approaching the top of the spiral stair. But there were no boards overhead, as there must once have been, and the spiral stair now led nowhere, if indeed it still existed behind the doorway.

It must be the wind, she told herself. Of course it was the wind, as surely it had been the other night! There were so many places open to the air at this end of the house, gaps where mortar had weathered away in unplastered walls, spaces where light showed through the ancient stone slabs of the roof. Even standing here she could feel the draughts.

Yet she didn't remember they'd ever been so bad as this, so fierce, so utterly chilling, as if somewhere out of sight the roof had opened fully to stormy skies. This was more than a draught, more like a gale, rushing down the hidden stairs towards her, a fierce chill blast of air ruffling her hair, stirring her clothes. So cold —!

The cold seeped into every part of her, into her very bones.

They were coming nearer, those footsteps, the creaking giving way to a light tapping sound…treading now on stone: stone steps, the steps of the spiral stair. Steadily, one by one, down, down they came towards the concealed doorway, towards the place where she stood.

Every impulse in her body warned her to turn and run for her life, but she could not move. The biting wind had frozen her, turned her body to ice, seized even her mind with a glacial hand. *I've got to go! I must! I must!*

Nothing moved, except the wind that swirled about her, and the approaching steps. She could only stand where she was, helpless, waiting. One —two—three—four, the steps descended, now only just out of sight, only one more turn of the stair—

Somewhere far behind her, at the further end of the house, the door to the yard clattered shut. With a sudden superhuman effort she wrenched herself away from where she stood, crossed the room, locked the door behind her and ran back towards the kitchen, slamming every intervening door as she went.

'Juliet! What on earth's the matter? You look as if you've seen a ghost!'

Leo, large as life, utterly normal, was standing there in the kitchen. Instinct told her to run to his arms and cling to him, as she had not done for months, not since—Instead she halted just a pace or two away. 'Where were you?'

'I went to fill up with petrol and get some more nails. Just got back.'

So it hadn't been Leo she'd heard. But then she already knew that. She shuddered. He put an arm round her, but only briefly, because she shook it off. 'Something's happened,' he said. 'Tell me!'

What had happened? How could she begin to tell him?

'No—nothing. I just thought I heard something, that's all.'

He studied her face, his expression questioning. She knew he didn't believe her, but after a moment he clearly decided to let it go. 'I'll give you a hand with the shopping.'

He carried the rest of the bags inside, while she made coffee for them both. 'Maybe we should get a dog,' he said as they sat at the table a little later. 'A bit of company for you when I'm out.'

'You know I don't like dogs.' She had been badly bitten as a small child and had never quite overcome her subsequent fear.

'All right, a cat. Something.'

'I'm fine. I just got a bit cold, that's all.'

He sat gazing at her, saying nothing, and then began to talk about a problem he had with the bathroom taps. Once, long ago, he would not so easily have let the matter drop. He would have known she was troubled, been certain of it, and persisted until he'd found out the reason why. Now the barrier that had been erected between them by Luke's death kept them from reaching out to one another.

Chapter Five

Jessie Maclaren rubbed her bruised side and edged her way with the help of the furniture towards her armchair by the fire. She would have liked to light the fire—she was beginning to feel cold—but it had taken every ounce of her remaining strength to get as far as the chair. She could do no more, not yet anyway.

She leaned back and closed her eyes. As the mist of confusion cleared, her mind scrolled back through the years, and she was a girl again, running through the fields with her cousin Sheila—long dead by now—delighted to be outstripping her, pulling ever further ahead, though Sheila was the older by two months. She could still recall her delight in her own strength and energy. She had been good at sports, good at many things.

But her father had died when she was in her teens and her mother had been an invalid for many years and, dutiful daughter that she was, she'd stayed at home to care for her. Her mother had died just as the world was engulfed in war, freeing her to join the Wrens, where she'd discovered new and unsuspected skills in herself, new friendships, and in time met handsome, serious-minded Captain Donald

Maclaren, who had offered her eventual security and the hope of a future, of children, of loving companionship. Yet she had never again been as happy as in those days when she ran through the fields and all of life lay ahead of her.

And now she would never run again. So many things she would never now do! In any case she had long ago lost all ambition, all hope for the future. What after all was there to show for her eighty-eight years of life? A fine son, certainly, and grandchildren, but nothing else at all that she could think of. However you looked at it, she had little time left now, for anything, even had she hoped to achieve much more. Sometimes she thought the end could not come soon enough, weary as she was, frightened, often in pain. Yet she didn't want life to finish like this, fizzling out in aimless dependency. She was a burden to those she loved—a worry at best—when all she wanted was a little richness in her life, some kind of purpose; and to feel both loved and cherished. Did anyone feel like that about the old, that they loved them so much that to lose them would hurt? Her mother had said once, on one of her very bad days, that no child loves her mother as a mother loves her child, and Jessie had been pierced by a sudden cruel vision of a cascade of love pouring unreturned down the generations. Yet later, newly mother of Alastair, she had not really believed it, though admitting that her feelings for her own mother had certainly been less loving than those her mother had for her. Now she knew her mother had only been stating an obvious truth.

Or was it simply that she was an unloveable person, that in old age her more agreeable characteristics had disappeared as her disappointment with what life offered had increased?

Suddenly she felt tears press against her closed lids and made herself swallow hard, forcing them back with a surge of anger at her weakness. She had never been a woman for tears. She was not going to begin now.

She opened her eyes and got slowly to her feet, stooping to turn on the gas fire before sitting down again. That had tired her, but at least she'd done it, and there had been no ill effects. The sudden strange sensation that had caused her to fall, without realising she had done so until she found herself lying on the floor at the bottom of the stairs—that had passed now. Thank goodness she had reached the final step before she fell! If it had happened anywhere near the top of that steep flight she would surely have been badly hurt. But now, back in her comfortable chair, she felt perfectly normal, if a little tired.

Please God, don't let it happen again! she prayed. Did prayer do any good? She had prayed a good deal in her life, but looking back it seemed to her that her prayers had gone largely unanswered—prayers that Alastair should marry that nice quiet girl from Dundee he'd met on holiday in the year before he went to university, prayers that Donald should recover from the prostate cancer that had killed him, prayers that she should get her strength and energy back in full after she broke her hip in a fall four years ago; prayers that Rosalind would suddenly realise what was expected of a dutiful daughter-in-law and agree to move to Scotland to be nearer to her mother-in-law, even perhaps move with Alastair into *Kenilworth*, the fine house Jessie had loved in Morningside, where they could all have lived together. There she'd had a circle of good friends, a routine, an agreeable social life, all of which she'd left behind when the house was sold. She had prayed too that Alastair would love her as deeply as she loved him, but that prayer too had failed. God had failed her, along with everyone else. She was deeply disappointed in Him.

Once, when she had ventured to put just a little of all this into words, her neighbour Nurse Hutchinson (who did not believe in God) had said briskly, 'Well, at least you have grandchildren!' Phyllis Hutchinson had never even married, so she had no one, though she was very rich in friendship and had an active social life—and good health, of course, as Jessie had not. 'You should learn to count your blessings. That's what I do if I get down: last thing at night I think of five good things that happened that day. You'll be amazed how cheering it is.'

She had tried it, once. But it had only brought home to her how blessed Miss Hutchinson was, in contrast to her. She could not even manage two good things, and they'd both been things that hadn't been as bad as she'd feared: it hadn't rained, so she'd got the washing dry, and her grandson Josh hadn't brought that black woman back to England with him, because she'd died. It was sad for Josh, of course, but she'd been amazed that anyone could have imagined such a mixed marriage would work. And at least it had meant that Josh was back in Meadhope and she could see him fairly often, if not quite as often as she would have liked. He was her favourite of her two grandchildren, Sophie being too brisk and spiky for her comfort, too like her mother. That was acceptable in a man, of course, but undesirable in a woman—an old-fashioned view perhaps, but there was nothing wrong with that.

Jessie was distracted by the sound of the post thudding on the mat, and made her way slowly to pick it up, hoping against hope there would be something really interesting, something she could open with excitement or eager anticipation.

She found a sheaf of leaflets advertising local takeaways and cut price stores, a letter from her bank offering her a loan (she had never owed money in her life, apart from the modest mortgage with which she and Donald had paid for their house), a catalogue from a mail-order firm she'd once bought a jumper from—poor quality too and long since worn out, so she'd no wish to patronise them again—and a reminder that her house insurance was due. No letters from friends, nothing personal or cheering. But then most of her friends were long dead, or shut up in nursing homes with only their delusions for company.

That was how life ended, with a fading of all that had given joy, the shrinking of horizons—

and goodness knows, hers had been narrow enough over the years, with little room for shrinkage!—the increase of infirmity and very likely the loss of mental faculties too. Just a burden on those she yearned to be loved by, that was all she was. There was nothing at all left for her to look forward to.

She carried her post through to the kitchen and slipped the bulk of it into the recycling bin, propping the insurance letter on the table for Alastair to deal with when he next looked in. She decided to help time pass a little less sluggishly by making a cup of tea and carrying it, together with two biscuits (her favourite ginger nuts) to her fireside chair. That would keep her going until she could decently start on cooking her dinner. Meanwhile, perhaps there was something on television that she could bear to watch. She flicked on the remote and channel-hopped until she alighted on an auction show, with a family clearing their loft of junk in the hope of raising enough for a holiday. *Nobody wants to work hard or save for anything these days,* she thought sourly, but she went on watching all the same, feeling pleasurably vindicated when the auction failed to raise the hoped-for amount.

When the programme ended, with still an hour to go to midday, she remembered that she was running low on cereal. Until a week or two ago she would simply have set out after lunch with her shopping trolley and bought it for herself at Meadhope's rather unappealing little convenience store. But since she'd begun to experience these strange 'turns' she'd grown increasingly afraid to go out. What if she should fall over in the street? Would people think she was drunk? Would someone in authority insist she went into hospital—or worse, into a home?

She went through to the hall and dialled Alastair's work number. 'I'm out of cornflakes,' she told him. 'Please pick some up for me on your way home.' She tried very hard not to hear the exasperation in his compliant response. Duty, that was what would make him do it, not love nor concern. But that was just the way it was, the way it had to be. Nothing she did or said could change it. She had not, of course, said anything to Rosalind or Alastair about the falls (though she had not been able to hide them all), still less about her fears. Rosalind—so brisk, so unfailingly energetic, so self-reliant—how she would despise her mother-in-law's increasing feebleness!

That night, Juliet woke again, into the dark. What had disturbed her? There was no creaking this time, no footsteps, nothing that she could hear.

Yes, there was—*there, now!*—not footsteps, but a faint distant sound like sobbing. The wind? She listened again. It was becoming clearer, more distinct, and it was surely, without doubt, the sound of someone weeping bitter tears.

Leo? Leo, alone in his room, remembering Luke, weeping for what they had lost, for his part in it, weeping as she herself had wept so often, in a helpless agony of grief without hope of resolution or consolation? There in the night she felt an unaccustomed surge of compassion, even of hope that now at last they might weep together, sharing their loss.

She switched on the light, pulled on her white towelling robe, slipped her feet into velvet mules and opened the door onto the landing. The sobbing was clearer now, louder, more anguished than ever. Could it be Leo? It seemed to come from somewhere to her left, but that couldn't be the case, for there was nothing there, only the solid wall of the ancient tower with its high vaulted roof. The sound must have come from the other direction, from beyond the closed door of Leo's room. She hurried along the landing and pushed open the door. 'Leo?'

It wasn't him. The room was quiet, though she could still hear the sobbing, further away, out there. She was about to retreat, when she heard a murmur from the bed. 'Mm?'

Maybe he wouldn't wake properly. She drew back; then saw him sit up, heard him grope around. Light flooded the room. 'Juliet? What's wrong?' Dazzled by the lamp, he rubbed his eyes.

'I thought I heard something.' She could hear it still. 'There! Listen!' She fell silent, while he listened, his expression increasingly puzzled.

'What am I supposed to be hearing?'

'Sobbing...There! Now!'

'Sobbing? What are you talking about?'

'Come over here—listen!'

Muttering under his breath, he joined her in the doorway, his head tilted to one side. 'I can't hear anything. What *is* the matter with you?'

'It's stopped now. But I heard it, truly I did. Sobbing, terrible sobbing. I thought it was you.'

'Well, it wasn't. So go back to bed.' He saw how she was shivering, even though it wasn't especially cold, and his voice softened. 'You really believe you heard something, don't you? You know these old houses—full of weird noises. Probably the wind, or mice in the roof. Or bats. Could be anything.'

'It was sobbing.'

'It was your imagination. Or a dream.' He put an arm about her but she shook it off. 'Would you like me to come in with you?'

She was tempted, but after a moment said, 'No thank you. I'm fine. I don't want to share a bed with someone who thinks I'm deluded.'

'I don't think you're deluded. Just mistaken. Sounds can't hurt you, you know.'

'Go back to bed then.'

Back in her room she wished she had not so hastily refused Leo's offer. She left the light on and pulled the duvet over her ears. Then the sobbing started again, clearly, unmistakably. With shaking hands she reached for the little box of earplugs that from habit she kept on the bedside table, for the few occasions when Leo was beside her and snoring. Once the foam filled her ears silence enveloped her, and she slept.

'It wasn't my imagination, what I heard,' she told Leo over breakfast. 'It stopped when I put earplugs in.'

'That only means it really was just mice, or the wind.'

She persisted, desperate that he should believe her, trying by the force of her own certainty to make him accept that what she'd heard was real.

It didn't work. He heard her with increasing impatience, then broke out, 'Oh for goodness sake, Juliet, common sense should tell you there's some perfectly rational explanation! And the most self-evident one I can think of is that you're under stress. Natural enough, perfectly excusable, but it can make for disturbing manifestations. That has to be it. First you smell non-existent roses, then you hear things! You should see a doctor.'

'Don't be ridiculous! I don't need a doctor. I'm not imagining it. I know what I heard.'

'What do you suggest then? An exorcist?' There was a world of sneering in his tone. 'Oh come on now, Juliet, there's got to be a sensible explanation for all this!'

'Which is that I'm not rational. I'm mentally disturbed. That's what you're saying, isn't it?'

'If you hear noises and I don't, then they're not out there but inside—in your head. Seems clear to me.' She was about to protest again, when he said briskly, 'Anyway, I haven't time to waste on your spectral imaginings. I've got to get onto BT again and get our broadband sorted out. You'd have thought by now they'd have got it up and running. It's beyond a joke. All I get on the end of the line is imbeciles who have no idea what I'm talking about and can't explain anything properly.'

She was irritated that he took her terrors so lightly as to be distracted by something so trivial as a broadband connection. 'Get someone in to sort it out for you then! That's what you always used to do.'

'Unnecessary expense—or what should be unnecessary expense, if people would only do the job properly in the first place. Besides, who do I ask? All one gets in the Yellow Pages are names. No indication of competence.'

'Rosie might know someone.' She saw his blank look. 'Rector, at Meadhope. I used to go to school with her. She called here the other day. I told you.'

'Oh, her! You can try her, if you like.' He moved restlessly about the kitchen. 'Is there any more coffee?'

Later, when he'd gone back upstairs to swear at his unresponsive computer, Juliet, having watched him go with exasperation, sat on at the table, staring gloomy and unseeing across the room. Was he right? Could she have imagined it all, the footsteps, the sobbing? Goodness knows, she had reason enough to grieve, and life had certainly been deeply stressful for a long time now, and she'd had no help from doctor or counsellor since Luke died. Then neither had Leo—and he'd never tried to talk to anyone about his feelings, as far as she knew. She at least had talked to her friends, or those she'd thought were her friends. Not that it had helped, but she'd tried, and she knew it had been obvious to everyone how stricken she was.

Leo had shown so little emotion that she'd wondered sometimes if he felt anything at all. Yet there had been those unexplained absences. She had been sure they were connected with Luke's death, though any attempt to get him to talk about it had been met with silence or a deft change of subject. Then, the suddenness with which he had given up his job and begun to talk of turning his back on the past, of leaving London far behind—didn't that show that there was something he wanted, *needed*, to leave behind? She too had seen a glimmer of hope in that decision.

Was she wrong? Had it been a ghastly mistake to come here, to leave everything familiar and cast out into a new life? The moment they'd seen the house, she'd been absolutely sure, convinced that this was the place for them, that here everything would be as well as it ever could be without Luke. It had felt like home, even in its rundown near-derelict state. Here, she'd believed, they could live and work and—eventually—end their days, with some sort of purpose, some sort of life together built up out of the ruins of this house and the ruin of their lives.

Yet last night it had felt nothing like the home she'd dreamed of. She shivered, recalling the footsteps, the sobbing, the sense of terror. But—*'Sounds can't hurt you,'* Leo had said, which was surely true; and already the memory was beginning to fade with the daylight.

A little later, stepping into the garden with her final mug of coffee, she felt enfolded in peace, refreshed by the beauty around her. It might not yet be home, but given time...

Later that day, Juliet rang Rosalind. She told her friend about Leo's technical difficulties, all the time wishing that she could instead tell her about the unexplained scent of roses, the night sounds, the things that were uppermost in her mind. But she made no mention of them, only had a matter-of-fact discussion with Rosalind which resulted in an offer of Josh Mclaren's services, as a currently inactive and unemployed computer expert.

'I'll give him a try then,' Leo said grudgingly when she told him. 'But I don't hold out any great hope. If that doesn't work I'm changing my broadband provider.'

Soon afterwards, frustrated at not being able to work on his computer as he'd intended that day, by moving funds they needed into a more accessible account, Leo drove away to look for a prop with which to support the archway of the hidden door, which he hoped to open up in the next few days. With a sense of relief, Juliet abandoned her dutiful scraping at the dining room plaster, changed into different old clothes and slipped out into the garden, where she gathered tools and set to work weeding and digging. All traces of fear and unease fell from her. Here, she felt at home, at peace, almost happy, in the positive way that was such a rare thing these days.

As she worked, she could see the garden take shape in her mind's eye. It would be as she had seen it in her dream, planted with low box hedging, its geometrical formality softened by the roses that bloomed in its beds, with other flowers among them, and herbs too—*parsley, sage, rosemary and thyme*, as the song had it. She was a little vague about these, but the roses— oh, there was no doubt there! They would be old roses, the sort that the lady of her dream would have grown, heady with scent, glowing with colour.

She kept an eye on her watch and as soon as there was any possibility that Leo would be home, put the tools away—cleaning them thoroughly to remove all trace of recent use— and went indoors. She stuffed her gardening clothes into a bin bag, which she hid at the back of her wardrobe, took a shower, and then went to do some more plaster-removing, so that she should be covered in grey dust and not earth when Leo came in. *Just like an alcoholic, hiding the evidence of secret drinking*, she thought with amusement: *I'm an addict, a gardening addict!*

Leo had clearly had a successful morning. Juliet, assembling a salad for lunch, looked up as he came into the kitchen and caught the pleased expression on his face. 'You look smug,' she said. Her heart gave an irrational twist of fear at the acknowledgement that this indicated he'd got his prop.

Then she saw he was carrying something that was clearly not a prop: a sturdy cardboard box, with handles, from which a faint sound emerged. He set it on the table. 'Here, for you! Thought it might stop those pesky mice disturbing your sleep—not to mention eating our biscuits.' They'd quickly learned not to leave uncovered food about in the kitchen.

Juliet watched, puzzled, as he opened the box. The noise from inside grew louder, a scratching sound, and what was definitely a faint mew. 'What have you—? Oh!'

Round blue eyes looked up at her. She could not resist. She reached into the box and lifted out the fluffy tabby kitten. 'Oh, he's so cute! Or is it a she?'

'He, they assured me. We'll need to get him neutered in due course, or he'll spray smells all over the place. But for now—well, I'm afraid it'll probably be a while before he's much of a mouser. They said to keep him in for a day or two until he's settled. He's guaranteed fully house trained, and I even had the forethought to buy a cat litter tray and all the paraphernalia you'll require. Call him a house-warming present if you like, a bit late.'

She knew what he was doing: bringing her a distraction, something to take her mind off strange noises in the night, on the assumption that they were all figments of a disordered imagination. Well, for now at least the strategy was working. How could it not, with such an adorable little creature snuggling into her arms? 'I'll have to think of a name for him.'

'I'll go and get the rest of the stuff. I guess

he'd like some milk.'

Juliet put milk in a saucer on the floor, and the kitten nudged it with his nose and then began eagerly to lap; the milk was gone in moments. When she picked him up again he purred so loudly that she felt his small body vibrate with the roar of it. 'You're a little tiger,' she murmured, rubbing her face against the soft fur. 'My little tiger.'

Looking up as Leo returned from the car, she caught an expression on his face that was both wistful and full of longing, as if he wished she would offer him a fraction of the affection she was lavishing on this new arrival in her life. *Tough!* she thought. *You don't get back under my skin so easily!*

But she relented enough to smile and thank him.

Chapter Six

By now, after years of practice, Alastair Maclaren could have produced Sunday lunch with his eyes closed and his mind on other things: joint (usually a chicken) in a low oven first thing, self-basting with wine, garlic and fresh herbs; potatoes into the hot upper oven as soon as he got in from church; dessert—a fruit crumble or pie—prepared a day or two before and then heated up (if necessary) at the last minute, vegetables prepared in the intervals between making the gravy and laying the table. By the time Rosalind was home, everything would be ready.

In recent years there had been the added complication of Jessie Maclaren, who always came back to the rectory after the morning communion service, but a small glass of sweet sherry by the sitting room fire usually kept her happy while she waited, especially if Josh was in a mood to keep her company until lunch was ready.

'You weren't in church this morning,' she reproached her grandson on this particular Sunday, as she did almost every week, a kind of automatic response to his kiss.

'No, Gran. Did I miss a treat?' He was

aware that teasing on such matters was a risky strategy, but was confident she loved him enough to forgive his irreverence.

'A treat, as you call it, would necessitate a sermon. As I have told your mother many times.'

'Mum always says that you can say all that has to be said in ten minutes. Anything more is waffle.'

'I know that is your mother's view. A sermon cannot be preached in ten minutes. That is not a sermon. There is no meat in it. Half an hour would give one something to take home and ponder.'

A sore bum, thought Josh, but knowing that would be a remark beyond the bounds of what was acceptable even from him, he kept the thought to himself. He knew from his father that not everyone of Presbyterian upbringing shared his grandmother's view of long sermons. She might miss them since coming to live in Meadhope, but Alastair Maclaren had been very glad to leave them behind when he married into the Anglican church.

Within half an hour they were sitting about the table in the dining room, enjoying the food —even Josh was eating well, Rosalind noted happily. He looked more cheerful too. Was the prospect of some sort of work already making him feel less lost and adrift?

'How are you getting to Holywell tomorrow?' Alastair asked him.

Josh cast a sideways glance at his mother. 'I'll get the bus. The two o'clock one should be fine.'

'It's a fair walk from the bus stop.'

'Do me good. Bit of exercise.'

'I am sure your mother will give you a lift,' said Jessie.

Josh exchanged a grin with his mother. 'Must think of the planet, Gran,' he said.

'What nonsense! In my view, all this talk of global warming is a confidence trick. There have always been fluctuations in the weather.'

'But your generation are the ones who set us an example,' Josh pointed out. 'You never waste anything. Isn't it good the younger generation are taking it on board?'

'That's simply common sense. But this cycling and walking everywhere—and a pony and trap! Whatever next! You will make yourself a laughing stock!'

That remark was addressed, pointedly, to Rosalind. 'The pony and trap idea was a bit of a joke,' she said. 'And I only use the bike if it's sensible to do so. It isn't always possible. No good dripping wet clothes all over the carpet when I'm doing sick visiting or whatever.'

'I think a pony and trap was a great idea,' said Josh. 'Just think of the publicity for the church! And kids would love it. All that muck for the gardens too!'

'Joshua, we are eating!'

'Sorry, Gran!'

'How are your dahlias doing?' Rosalind asked hastily, trying to move the conversation on to something uncontroversial.

'Well enough. But I do need some help with the garden. Perhaps Joshua would like to come and give an afternoon to the weeding.'

Josh, who hated gardening, said quickly, 'I don't think I'd do, Gran. I don't know a weed from a flower.'

'I would supervise. You would only have to do as I instructed.' She finished the last of her roast parsnips—her favourite vegetable—and laid her knife and fork neatly side by side on her plate. 'The fresh air would be very good for you. You're looking more than a little peely wally.'

That Scots expression was one Rosalind loved when it came from Alastair, yet with the complex illogicality of family relationships, found irritating from her mother-in-law. But she bit back the protest on the tip of her tongue—*Josh is fine; leave him alone!*—and confined herself to grinning sympathetically at her son. After all, he wasn't fine, was he?

'Let's see how much work Josh has to do on the Holywell computers before we start burdening him with gardening as well,' Alastair said mildly. 'Perhaps you should find a gardener who'll give it a thorough once-over.' Before his mother could retort—as he knew she would—that one should not have to pay others when family members were available, he went on, 'Has everyone finished? There's pear and chocolate tart if anyone's got any room.'

Why did people tinker with computers when they had no idea what they were doing? Josh wondered. He was seated at Leo's magnificent desk, placed so that it looked out over the green valley, the trees lining the river, the hills beyond: the desk of someone who knew that his work was important, that *he* was important.

'There's a great deal still to be done in here,' Leo had said as he'd shown him into the study, with its neatly labelled packing cases ranged against one wall, 'but so long as I can get the broadband working then I've enough to be going on with. I've never had this trouble before. It should be a simple matter to transfer the connection from one property to another.'

'Don't worry. I'll get it sorted,' Josh had promised, relieved when Leo had finally ceased trying to explain all the different things he'd tried and left him to get on with it. It wasn't the broadband provider, of course (well, not 'of course'—there were frequently problems with them, but not this time); it was Leo, who was used to having someone in his employment who dealt with anything to do with computers, yet thought his own knowledge was by now sufficient for him to manage without help, as a result of which he'd caused a whole set of interconnected problems. This sort of attitude used to infuriate Josh, as he struggled to untangle the mess some know-all novice had created. Now he simply felt weary. It wasn't after all that important, in the general scale of things. And it gave him something to do. But he still wondered at the capacity for people to be prepared to tackle a task for which they were manifestly unqualified.

There was though, he had to admit, something satisfying about resolving a problem, especially when it was complex and difficult; yet one you knew you *would* be able to resolve, given time and perseverance. It was an activity without emotion, cerebral, calming. It shut out pain.

He was deep in concentration when he heard the door open behind him. 'Josh? I've brought you a coffee.' Juliet set it down on the slate coaster protecting the desk's surface, a small plate of biscuits beside it. He thanked her. 'How's it going?'

'OK so far. What time is it?'

'Half past four.'

He'd been working for two hours then. It hadn't felt like it. It was a long time since he'd known time pass so quickly.

Juliet propped herself against one of the stacks of packing cases. 'We've just heard— we're having a visitor next week. Our first house guest.'

He wished she'd go away and let him get on with the work. He didn't want to listen to chat, to think carefully how to respond to it, to have to consider someone else's feelings. He knew from his mother that Juliet had her grief too, but his own was enough for the time being, more than enough. He wanted to be allowed to put it aside for a time, as he had been doing; to forget himself completely. 'Mm?'

'Katie was Luke's girlfriend. She's such a lovely girl. His—what happened—shocked her so much. There's been no one else for her since. We didn't know her so well, before…But now she feels like one of the family. Anyway, she's coming to stay for a few days. She's working now, in a salon in Marylebone High Street, but she has some holiday due, so she's asked if she can come and see us. I'd been so afraid we'd lose touch when we moved, so this is very good news. Something to look forward to.'

He tried to make suitable polite murmurings, but perhaps she sensed that he was less than interested, for she said suddenly, 'Well, I'd better let you get on. Just give a shout if there's anything you need.'

It was good coffee—he was beginning to appreciate such things again—and the biscuits were those delicious homemade ones from the café in the market place, melting in the mouth, studded with chocolate and nuts. He felt regret for his churlishness towards Juliet. She seemed a nice person, and she'd lost someone too. She deserved better.

When he emerged again from his work, with the chief problems solved and only some minor tidying up to do, it was beginning to grow dark. He hadn't really registered how the nights were drawing in, now that they were well into October.

There was a rattle of rain on the windows— he could scarcely see anything out there now—

and the wind was getting up. He hoped Leo would give him a lift home when he was ready. Surely he would? It was a long walk to the bus, and they were only every two hours at this time of day. Anyway, he hadn't quite finished.

Somewhere, far off in the depths of the house, a door banged, then again and again. The wind was making a dreary howling noise. Or was it the wind? It sounded almost human.

Funny what the imagination could do. Old houses had all kinds of strange noises. Anyway, it had stopped…

No it hadn't. There it was again. Distinctly, unmistakably: not wind, not an animal, but a human sound, a howling that came from utter despair. So he had howled, inwardly, as Miriam lay dying, as she'd slipped away from him, beyond his reach; as he'd faced a future without her. This had been the sound wrung from his very soul, though never out loud like this.

He could see her now, her beautiful mahogany skin drenched with sweat, stretched over the dramatic bones of her face; all laughter gone, all light, all hope…Then the moment when he knew: when she, the essential Miriam, his love, his life, wasn't there any more, but had slipped away, leaving an empty husk that held only her superficial shape, that was not her.

He pushed back the chair, stood up. The sound caught at his heart, cried to him for help, for consolation. He went to the door and wrenched it open.

Nothing. Nothing at all. Not even the sigh of the wind. He stared out onto the dark landing, trying to make out something, anything, any sight or sound to explain what he'd heard. He felt shaken, disturbed.

The landing light snapped on. It all looked utterly normal, with Juliet coming into sight up the stairs, the kitten dancing at her heels. 'I thought you might like to stay for supper,' she said. 'Then Leo will run you home.' He realised the air was full of good cooking smells; and that he was hungry. It all seemed very ordinary.

She scooped up the kitten. 'Tiger, you're not allowed upstairs! We're not one hundred per cent sure he's properly house-trained yet,' she explained to Josh. Then she must have seen something disturbing in his face. 'Are you all right?'

'I'm fine,' he said. 'There are some creepy noises in this house though. Especially with all this wind. Old houses, I suppose.'

She was silent, scrutinising him in a way that told him she was not taking his words as lightly as he had expected her to. 'What did you hear?'

Should he just make light of it, pretend it was nothing? He sensed that she would not believe him, that she already knew that there was more to his words than they implied on the surface. 'It sounded like someone sobbing.'

'So you heard it too.' She spoke almost in a whisper, her tone a mixture of relief and fear. 'I've thought I was imagining it. Leo never hears anything. But I do. Three times now.'

'Just now? Did you hear it just now?'

'No. It's usually been late in the night or very early morning. It comes from the old part of the house.'

'I thought it was all old?'

'The mediaeval bit, the old pele tower—that's the bit with the hall. This part's only eighteenth century, we think.'

'Only!'

'Oh, we get blasé about such things, you know. What's a mere two hundred or so years when you've the best part of a thousand to play with?' She smiled, suddenly looking much younger. 'You don't know what a relief it is to know it wasn't just me. I didn't believe it was, but you begin to doubt, when you're the only one to hear things.'

'And now you're over the moon to know for sure that you live in a haunted house!'

'Yes,' she admitted wryly, 'that does sound a bit crazy. But better a haunted house than thinking you're going mad. Tell me, did you have any idea about the person sobbing— whether it was a man or a woman, for instance?'

'Oh, a woman. I'm sure.' Josh, conscious how foolish that sounded, laughed. 'No idea why, but I'm quite sure.'

'Yes, me too. And I believe it was the woman in my dream.' She told him then about the scent of roses in the garden, and the dream that followed it. 'But she wasn't unhappy then. I thought she was just wanting me to restore the garden.' She laughed unsteadily. 'Maybe I *am* going mad after all!'

'Only if I am too. If you'd told me about this yesterday I'd have thought you were bonkers. But not now, not after what I heard. We can't both have imagined it—can we?'

'Certainly not! And now perhaps Leo will believe me. He thinks it's stress, grief. Because of Luke. But you, just a normal healthy young man, no hang-ups—that's different.'

'Not entirely.' His voice was soft, reluctant. 'My wife died. It's just over a year.'

'Oh.' For a moment she looked more disappointed than sympathetic, though she recovered enough to say, 'I'm so sorry!' Before going on, 'But I'm afraid Leo will think you're a tainted witness too. I'm sorry, that sounds very unfeeling.'

'I know what you mean.' He gave a rueful smile. 'But I know, as you do, that I wasn't imagining it.'

'You'd have thought if this house was haunted we'd have heard something from somebody. The estate agent or the solicitor perhaps.'

'Maybe they hushed it up. Not everybody wants to share their home with a ghost.'

'I certainly don't want one who sobs all night. A lady who loves her garden—that's one thing. This is something else altogether.'

Josh was silent, but his expression caused Juliet to prompt him, 'What are you thinking?'

'Perhaps there really was someone once, who lived here; someone who had a great grief —or did something terrible that she really regretted afterwards, something really bad.' He looked at her earnestly. 'This woman in your dream—what did she look like? What sort of clothes?'

'Oh I don't know! Something long and black.' She thought hard, and then shook her head. 'No, it's—Hang on, I'll draw her.' She put the kitten on the floor, pulled a note pad towards her and began to draw, her pencil moving with swift emphatic lines. Josh watched as a slight figure emerged, saw the full skirts, the gown over them, the ruff, the distinctive hood.

'She looks kind of Elizabethan. Can I take this?'

'Of course. But what will you do with it?'

'I'm not sure. Maybe first off, I'll see if I can find a costume book—or check if there's something on the internet. If I can find out when she lived, then maybe I'll have some idea where to start looking for clues as to who she was.'

'You're serious, aren't you?'

'Do you think I'm the one who's mad?'

'No—no, of course not. I'm just not sure what you expect to find.'

'Nor am I. But it'll be fun to do a bit of research into the history of the house. Something to do. If you don't mind—or would you rather do it yourself?'

'Oh, I've enough to do as it is. No, you have a go. I'll look forward to hearing what you find out.' Then she added, 'One thing though— don't tell Leo what you're doing. He really *will* think we're mad. So be discreet, keep it low key.' She retrieved the kitten from a far corner of the room. 'Come on you! Back to where you belong!' Then, to Josh, 'Supper will be about half an hour.'

'I had a visit from Peter Lewis today,' Rosalind told Alastair as they got ready for Jeremy Wynyard's fiftieth birthday party at Ashburn Hall; Alastair was only just in from work. 'On his way back from visiting family in Scotland—you know he has an aunt in Arbroath? He decided to call in, just on impulse.'

'How is he?'

'Not happy. Oh, personally he's all right—he and Sammy are together for life, if anyone is. No, it's the new vicar at St Cuthbert's.' St Cuthbert's Coldwell was the church where Rosalind had served until coming to Meadhope six years before.

'I thought what's-his-name had left. Or been encouraged to move elsewhere, as you so kindly put it.'

'He has. This is the new one.'

'Not another disaster!'

'I'd heard good things of him from others. But apparently he's been preaching against the sin of Sodom and told Peter in so many words that if he continued to live with Sammy he couldn't receive communion.'

'That's appalling!'

'Isn't it? Anyway, Peter's started going to St Oswald's instead. But he's finding it a wrench.'

'No wonder.'

'He's been part of St Cuthbert's nearly all his life, and contributed a huge amount in a quiet way. Sometimes I despair of the Church of England! How can we preach a loving God —?' She caught Alastair's eye and grinned. 'Sorry! I won't go on.'

'Not this time anyway!' He buttoned up his shirt. 'Oh, by the way, how did Josh get on over at Holywell?'

'He's still there. Must have been a more difficult problem than he thought.'

'Or Juliet Marston has induced him to stay for supper.'

'That's the most likely. I expect she's a cordon bleu cook.' She turned so that Alastair could zip up her dress—the stereotypical little black dress, which fortunately showed off her still-bright hair to perfection. 'Maybe this will revive his interest in computers.' She laughed. 'I never thought I'd hear myself say that! Remember how we used to despair of his having any normal interests, how he used to go on and on about computers?'

'I do indeed. It's seared into my very soul! Sad to think that now it would seem like a positive development. It might even help him find something useful to do with himself, long-term.'

'To be honest, I rather doubt that simply working with computers is going to be enough for him now, after Africa. But we shall see. We always knew it would take time. And I think he's conscious he needs to be self-supporting. But we have to let it be for his own sake, not to save us paying for his keep.'

'That goes without saying.'

Rosalind's gaze suddenly focussed on her husband. 'You're not wearing that tie, are you?'

'What's the matter with it?' He glanced down at the purple and black stripes.

'Nothing at all, if you want to look as if you're going to a funeral.'

'That's how I feel. Should my attire not reflect that?'

She laughed and hugged him. 'Chin up! Be brave! Stiff upper lip old chap and all that! We're only going to a party!'

'Yes, indeed,' he said with exaggerated lugubriousness. 'Why could we not have used your day off as an excuse?'

'Because Daphne sees her party as a great

way for exhausted rectors and stressed librarians to relax, so she wouldn't have accepted the excuse. You know Daphne—once she's set on something—' She had dived into the wardrobe, leafing her way through Alastair's tie rack.

'I know I know! But an evening with the hunting set—not my idea of a good night out!'

Rosalind grinned. 'We only have to show willing for an hour or so. Hopefully stay long enough for some food and then leave.' She emerged from the wardrobe with a vibrantly colourful tie hanging from her fingers. 'This one —much better. Hurry up now!'

Ashburn Hall was alive with light and music when Rosalind and Alastair walked towards the classical front portico from the place where they'd (eventually) found to park the car on the road that led into the village.

They were greeted warmly in the hallway by Daphne, who then dragged them through two or three other rooms to where her son lurked in a relatively quiet corner talking to a plain young woman who looked oddly out of place—and sounded it too, for she spoke with a strong local accent that stood out among all the voices loud with echoes of the hunt. She slipped away into the crowd as soon as they appeared; Rosalind saw disapproval on Daphne's face, which perhaps explained it. 'Goodness knows who that was! Some gatecrasher!' She grasped her son's arm. 'Jeremy, you know Rosalind of course. Not sure if you've met Alastair, Meadhope's organist and choir master extraordinaire.'

Jeremy was a large, shy, red-faced man who yet somehow faded into whatever background he stood against. He muttered some sort of conventional greeting, and as soon as possible made his excuses and left them. By then his mother had moved away too. 'We'd better circulate,' Rosalind murmured. 'You know, Jeremy looks as uncomfortable as we are. I guess his mother selected the guests—they'll be her friends, not his.'

'Maybe that's because he hasn't any,' Alastair suggested. 'Poor man won't have had much chance to make friends, under his mother's thumb all his life.'

The evening was very heavy going. Rosalind knew some of those who were there, but most of them seemed to be from outside the parish, large noisy people talking about hunting, the iniquities of the Labour government and their high hopes for an early Conservative victory. Having extricated themselves from several such groups, Rosalind and Alastair came at last face to face with a middle aged woman who had a faint look of Daphne—a relation perhaps. 'Caroline Stanway,' she introduced herself. 'Sister of the birthday boy.'

Of course! Daphne's other child…They returned the introductions, and—to avoid horsey talk—asked Caroline about the house and its history. 'Your family's been here for generations, hasn't it?'

'Came over with the Conqueror, Mummy always says—bit of an exaggeration, but you get the picture. There've been Wynyards here for ever. Strictly of course Mummy's only been a Wynyard since she married, but you know her, never does things by halves. She's more Wynyard than Daddy ever was, more than Jeremy or I, come to that. Knows the place backwards, and its history. Like a look around?' They accepted gladly and were given a tour of the rambling building of various ages, along passages, up stairs, through countless rooms opening successively one into another.

'This reminds me a bit of Holywell,' Rosalind said. 'A friend of mine has just bought it.'

'Interesting house. About the same age, the oldest bit. Though of course it declined to a mere farmhouse round about the eighteenth century. Catholic stronghold before that, like a good many round here. As we were, until going over to the established church seemed a good strategic move. Too many penalties being Catholic. Good thing we did, or how would Ashburn church have survived without Mummy? Has your friend seen the ghost?'

'No—not that I know of. Is there one?'

'Oh, every old house has its ghost! Not that I've ever seen one here. Can you imagine a ghost standing up to Mummy?' She laughed. 'Ghosts, priests' holes, secret passages—any old house is supposed to have the lot. But I guess it's mostly wishful thinking.' She glanced at the grandfather clock standing in the corner of the room. 'Supper time, I think. Shall we investigate?'

The supper at least was good, a huge spread laid out on a vast table in the Hall's grand dining room. And once they had eaten their fill, Rosalind and Alastair were able to leave.

It was just after midnight when they reached home, to find Josh slumped in front of the television, though he switched it off as soon as his mother looked into the room. 'Wasn't really watching,' he said, getting up from the sofa. 'How was the party?'

There was something about his expression that disturbed Rosalind, always sensitive to her son's moods. She perched on the sofa's arm. 'Pretty dire, as we expected. How's the Holywell broadband? All sorted?'

'What—? Oh, that, yes. It's all working.' He stood in front of her, saying no more.

'What's wrong?'

'Nothing. Everything's fine…' Still he stood there; and then suddenly dropped onto the sofa beside her. 'Mum, have you ever heard anything about Holywell being haunted?'

'Haunted!' What a strange coincidence! She stared at him, remembering Caroline's words. Had there been more to them than they had thought at the time? Caroline's tone had been light, her expression sceptical. 'What makes you say that? Did you see something?'

'Not see, hear. Terrible sobbing, like someone's heart was breaking. Juliet's heard it too. Don't say anything, Mum, you mustn't, not to anyone! Juliet thought she was imagining it. Leo's not heard it at all. But there have been all sorts of strange things, she says.'

Rosalind told Josh what they'd heard from Caroline. 'We weren't sure if she was serious. Though you'd have thought if there really had been stories about a ghost they'd have heard about them before they bought the house. That sort of thing's usually well known. It can even help sell an old house.'

She saw Josh shudder. 'Not that, not what I heard,' he said with feeling. 'That would put you off.'

'Of course, the house has been empty for years, and before that old Fred Peart more or less lived in one room, the kitchen, I think.'

'That's one of the newer bits, isn't it? Could be he lived there because he didn't want to hear the noises, or see things.'

'Who's seeing things?' Alastair, already in his dressing gown, put his head round the door. 'Aren't you folks ever going to bed? Some of us have to get up in the morning.'

Rosalind, glancing first at Josh to make sure he had no objection, told Alastair what had happened.

'Sounds creepy.'

'What I heard isn't the whole of it.' He told them about the lady in the garden, and then pulled Juliet's drawing from his pocket.

'Late sixteenth century, at a guess,' said his father. 'Maybe a little later if she was old fashioned or hard up.'

'It's a bit weird isn't it, to be thinking of her as a real person, instead of someone in a dream? It doesn't make sense.'

'*There are more things in heaven and earth…*' murmured Rosalind.

'But one thing on earth that's only too real and certain is the alarm clock,' put in Alastair. 'At this rate it'll go off before we've got to bed. I suggest you get some sleep and then arrange to go and see Keith Grey.' Keith Grey had been churchwarden at St Luke's Meadhope for a good part of the previous decade. Long retired from his work for the local council, he had ample time to pursue his interest in local history and archaeology. 'He knows more about the history of Meadhope than anyone I can think of. He might at least give you some pointers as to where to start looking for answers, if there are any to be found.'

In the end, Juliet did tell Leo about Josh's research—up to a point, at least. That evening she'd fought an increasing reluctance to go to bed at all. If she'd been sure that there'd be no messes—if he'd been confined downstairs without mishap for a few more days—she would have taken Tiger upstairs with her, but it was still a little soon for that. She would have to rely on earplugs to protect her from the night sounds, and hope they were enough to allow her to fall peacefully sleep. She'd been glad to know from what Josh had heard that what she'd experienced had not after all been simply a figment of her troubled imagination, but that did not help her feel calmer when it came to going to bed. She knew now that what she'd heard was real; that there was some *thing*, some disturbing presence in this house. Shutting it out with earplugs, telling herself it could do her no harm, did not alter the fact that it was there.

She reached the landing just as Leo emerged from the bathroom. 'Goodnight, my dear.' He came to kiss her, the light perfunctory kiss that was generally the most she would allow.

But tonight she felt an unaccustomed tenderness towards him. He had been so thoughtful, giving her the kitten. Whatever anger there still was in her heart, she had to acknowledge that he cared about her. And she was afraid, going to a lonely bed...'Will you come in with me tonight? Please!'

He looked both startled and delighted. 'Of course! So long as you don't keep me awake with stories of spooky noises.'

'If you're beside me the only spooky sounds I'm likely to hear are your snores.'

Just for a moment, the little joke linked them, held them closer than they'd been for a long time. He even, briefly, risked sliding an arm about her. 'At least you know precisely where *they* come from.'

'Only too well!' As they got into bed, pulling up the duvet around them, Juliet found herself saying, 'You know Josh, who came today?'

'Hmm. Seemed to know what he was doing, I'm glad to say.'

'Yes, well—he was very interested in the house and its history.'

'So it seemed.' Josh had asked a number of questions about it over supper.

'He thinks he'd like to do some research, see if he can find out anything about the people who owned this house in the past.'

Leo put out the bedside light. 'Pity there was so little with the deeds. Be interesting to see what he comes up with. If anything.'

Lying in the dark with that unaccustomed presence at her side, Juliet felt a flutter of desire, enough for her to reach out and take Leo's hand. Encouraged, he rolled towards her and drew her to him, holding her, stroking her hair, kissing her. She felt herself respond, her breath quicken—and then clearly, unmistakably, came the heart-wrenching sound of sobbing. She was about to say, *'There! You must hear that!'* but stopped as the words rose to her lips. Leo would not have heard it, of that she was completely sure. Shuddering, she pulled herself out of his arms and reached for her earplugs, with a hasty, 'Goodnight!'—a clear signal that the moment of tenderness was at an end.

She hurried to push the earplugs into place, but her hands were trembling so much that she dropped one, and had to scrabble under the bed in the dark, trying to find it, desperate to shut out the noise.

Leo's irritation broke into her panic: 'What are you doing?'

'I've dropped an earplug.'

'Put the light on then.'

She did, with relief, found the earplug and pushed it into place. After that, she lay rigid at Leo's side, trying not to strain her ears for the least sound. His snoring, beginning soon afterwards, was loud enough to reach her, but though she heard nothing else, all sleepiness had left her, and there was no longer any companionable reassurance in Leo's presence beside her. She seemed unable to find a comfortable position, turning and turning from this side to that, first feeling too hot and pushing the duvet from her; then tugging it about her again as the chill of the room seeped into her body. Inevitably, though she'd tried not to disturb him, her restless wakefulness disturbed Leo. 'Can't you keep still? It's no good expecting me to share the bed if you keep me awake half the night.'

'The amount you've been snoring you haven't had much trouble sleeping.'

But he clearly had, for some time just before dawn he got up and announced that he was returning to his own peaceful bed, to catch up on sleep.

Chapter Seven

Rosalind had a funeral visit to make the following morning, the most difficult kind, to a couple whose baby had died after a few weeks of painful existence. She had somehow to steer her way through the combination of anguish, relief and guilt that was tearing them apart and offer the ordered rituals of consolation, in the hope that they might there find something to cling to in the only too immediate chaos of their universe. It took all her reserves of compassion, patience and restraint, all she had learned throughout her years of ministry, to bring things to a point where hymns and readings were chosen, music decided on, all the routine arrangements that were not routine at all, put in place for the day that would mark the ending of their son's brief life. She knew that even if in future another child was born to them—and there seemed to be no medical reason why not —this child and this time with all its pain would always be a part of their lives.

Walking home afterwards, glad of the fresh air, she thought of the loss of children, and how deeply it scarred the parents, how impossible it was ever to be recovered from; and then, by a logical progression, found herself thinking of

Juliet—and of what Josh had told them last night. All that talk of historical research, of trying to find out who had lived at Holywell hundreds of years ago, as if all of it was connected in truth to a real person—it could not mask the fact that something very strange, something altogether outside her experience had happened there yesterday.

She had never given much thought to ghosts, except as phenomena essential to certain kinds of story—gothic novels, or those disappointing children's stories where the ghost turned out to be someone dressing up, which had always left her feeling a bit cheated; or the old Hammer horror films for which she had a sneaking fondness. But this strange manifestation Josh had reported—she felt a shiver run up her spine even now, just thinking about it in broad daylight. Ghosts (outside films and story books) were up there with dubious relics, crystals, astrology and all the other irrational trappings that had always lurked on the fringes of what she regarded as true religious experience. She regarded herself as a rational person, though conscious that to an atheist any sort of spiritual belief was irrational, her own lively questioning faith included. If she had given any thought to what people meant by ghosts, it was to see them as figments of a troubled imagination, indications of some kind of psychological problem, arising often from a deeply hidden trauma in the person who had witnessed the 'ghost'.

And now not only her oldest friend, but also her own son claimed to have witnessed something that was beyond obvious and immediate explanation. Where did that leave her scepticism?

The only common thread was that both of them—the friend and the son—had suffered a cruel personal loss that could perhaps explain what they had heard. Certainly Rosalind acknowledged that any rational outside observer would clutch at that explanation. But she knew them both—one of them very well indeed—and that made a difference. She could not dismiss what they'd heard so easily, in the circumstances. Besides, they were very different people with different experiences of grief. That they should both hear the same thing in the same place on separate occasions—did that not indicate it was all rather more than a projection of a disordered mind?

It troubled her particularly that Josh should have experienced something of this kind, even though he seemed to be taking it in a positive way. He had not seemed so enthusiastic about anything for a long time as he had this morning, talking over breakfast about his forthcoming visit to Keith Grey and his hopes for this little piece of historical research. Yet did it all indicate something about his present mental state, something very disturbing at that?

As she crossed the Rectory garden she shrugged her thoughts away—nothing she could do about them anyway—and concentrated instead on the things that filled her diary for the rest of the day.

Josh made his way to Mill House the following morning, as arranged by an earlier phone call to Keith Grey. He'd been preparing what he was going to say as he went, the right words to elicit the information he wanted without betraying his reasons. Once in the snug lounge of the house, with a coffee at his elbow, he gave a careful reply to Keith's, 'Do I gather you have a local history query for me?'

'I was over at Holywell yesterday. It's a fascinating old house—'

'I've heard so. One of those many-layered places—lots of different periods. I'd love to take a look around it myself.'

'I'm sure they'd be happy to give you a tour,

though they're still in a bit of a mess. They've only just moved in. I was there to sort out a computer problem for them. But we got talking…The thing is, they don't know much about the history of the place. But it's such a fascinating old house; I thought I'd like to find out something for them. It's just the sort of place that should have a really exciting history —lots of evil deeds, a ghost of course, everything you'd expect.'

'I don't know about the evil deeds, though I think I did read somewhere that Holywell was said to have a ghost. But they tend to say that about every old house worth its salt—and Holywell is very old. Certainly there haven't been any recent stories of that kind, as far as I know. But then old Fred Peart wasn't given to socialising much and most of the house was shut up while he was there. The Marstons must have had an awful lot of clearing up to do before they could even begin to move in, I'd think.'

'They did.'

'But no ghosts?'

He hesitated for just a moment. 'No—no ghosts.' Sounds didn't count did they?

Keith grinned. 'There's time! Anyway, all I can suggest is that you do a bit of research if you want to know more. But in a place that old there's an awful lot of history and most of it won't be recorded I guess. You need a big name connected with a place for much to survive in the way of records. You're likely to have to cover a lot of ground to find a few nuggets of interest. Are you game for that?'

'I'd love to. But where do I start?'

'Well, maybe with any local history books you can lay your hands on. The county library has a good selection. That should keep you out of mischief—there are hundreds of them. They don't all have references, but if they have, follow up any that look promising. After that there are parish registers and rent rolls and court records; maybe even some national records. You could always start with Domesday Book!'

Josh laughed and made a stalling gesture with his hands. 'Stop! That's the rest of my life you've got mapped out by the sound of it! I only want to find out a bit, not everything there is to know.'

'Oh, it's addictive once you get started, believe me!'

'I'm not sure I want to get addicted. But I'll think about it. Thank you anyway.' He rose to his feet.

'Hang on a minute! You can borrow this.

Just to whet your appetite!' Keith reached up to the bookshelves that filled one wall and took down a battered green volume. *Meadhope Byways,* the title read. 'Very Victorian and amateurish, but it's got all the local stories. Though come to think of it, your best bet as a starting point is probably the Surtees Durham histories. You'll find them in the University Library.'

Josh thanked him, declined a second cup of coffee and walked back to the rectory, deep in thought. He was nearly there when he remembered he'd promised to call on his grandmother today. He did a swift about-turn and knocked on her door, to be greeted with a warmth she withheld from his parents, from his mother in particular.

'Ah, Joshua, you're just in time to take advantage of this fine weather! I'll show you what needs to be done.' So her welcome had not been fired simply by her love for her grandson!

Before he could protest, or say (as he'd meant to do) that he couldn't stay long, she'd led him round the back of the house and was pointing out the beds she needed weeding, indicating which were weeds and which flowers —though in fact he was a good deal more knowledgeable about such things than he'd led her to believe. The next thing he knew, he was bending over the bed forking out chickweed and shepherd's purse and staking his grandmother's prized dahlias.

'They should get Gran running the country,' he said ruefully to his mother when, aching and muddy, he at last made it home. 'She'd have everyone sorted in no time. She doesn't let you say no.'

'We had a Prime Minister like that once. Margaret Thatcher they called her.'

Josh knew quite well what his mother had thought of the Iron Lady. 'Oh, yes well—maybe not. OK if I have a hot bath? Otherwise I'll not be able to walk tomorrow.'

Much later, warmed and fed, he settled down to read the book Keith Grey had lent him. It was a long time since he had done any sort of concentrated study—not since he'd been a student, in those days now cut off from him by the dark abyss of Miriam's dying. But it felt good, to settle down at his small desk in his room—laptop pushed aside for once—and simply read a book. He had a pen and paper ready in case he found anything of interest.

The book had no index and no references, which made it rather frustrating as anything but an entertaining read, but he persevered—the style was lively enough for such an old book. By the end of an hour he'd found two references to Holywell: one stated that it was a property built on land given to a loyal supporter of an early Prince Bishop of Durham; the other, that it was among many estates in the Dale whose owners remained staunchly Catholic after the Reformation, Ashburn Hall being mentioned as another. Which was not much more than his mother had already told him. It would have to be the university library then…

How odd, he thought, to be seriously considering researching someone in a dream, as if they'd had a concrete existence! It made no sense at all—and yet it did not feel irrational somehow.

Chapter Eight

'I'll need a hand with that doorway today. I want to finish opening it up, now I've got the prop—can't wait to see what's behind it! But it's a two-man job—'

'Then get a man in!' Juliet snapped. Tiger slid from her hands and danced off after some imaginary prey. She envied him his animal carelessness.

'Oh, come now, Juliet, you can help me with this—it's not that hard! You surely haven't got anything else lined up for today?'

She shrank from the very thought of it. She had no wish at all to go anywhere near that part of the house today or any day. Who knew what dark forces they might disturb by opening the doorway onto those ancient stairs? What indeed had they already woken, released to find its way into their lives? It was surely significant that she'd first heard the steps in the night, the sobbing, after Leo had discovered the doorway. Until then, there had been only happy manifestations: the scent of roses, her lady in the garden.

She knew she could not begin to try and explain all this to Leo, so laying herself open to ridicule or (worse) further accusations of neurosis. And she could think of no valid excuse —no acceptable, *rational* excuse—for refusing what he asked. She had nothing planned, no other major call on her time, and besides, renovating the house was the whole purpose of buying it, their project for the future. She tried one last argument, one that he must surely see the sense in: 'You know I think we should leave it for now. There's plenty else to be done. It's just a frill, something we don't need, even if it's nice to have.'

'Juliet, you know how much this means to me! Once it's open, once we've seen what's there, what we're dealing with, then I'll give all the attention you like to the other rooms. Just humour me in this!'

She hesitated. Should she risk telling him she would have nothing to do with it; she had better things to do, he had his priorities wrong, and in this he was on his own? They would all be perfectly logical arguments, but he would be hurt and angry and uncomprehending, and as usual she wanted only to avoid any cause of conflict, whatever the cost. 'All right. I'll help.'

'You might sound a bit more enthusiastic.'

'I didn't have a very good night, that's all.' *The understatement of the decade—!* She'd put off going to bed as long as she could bear, and once there left the light on, reading until she fell asleep. And yet the sobbing, waking her a short time after, had been worse than ever. She'd had to resort to earplugs again.

She took her time getting ready in her old clothes (the indoor ones, with their coating of plaster dust, not the wholesome earth-smelling muddy garments left from her gardening episode) and then joined Leo in the great hall. She felt sick, her stomach churned, but she forced herself to take deep slow breaths. This had to be done; she had to face it somehow.

She stood rigid behind him, trying to listen intently as he told her what he wanted to do, how he planned to tackle the job. It took all her will power to keep still, to stay there.

'See here—the infill stuff is mostly rubble, so I guess the archway will hold. But just in case, I want to get this in place as soon as possible, to make certain it's properly shored up.' *'This'* was the massive adjustable metal prop he had brought home in triumph the other day. 'It's likely that the door surround will still hold everything in its place—you can see how beautifully made it is, a real craftsman's job— but we can't be sure. We shan't know until we have it cleared.' He turned to pat her on the shoulder. Encouragement—? Reassurance—? It didn't help. 'Now, masks on! This'll be dusty work.' He handed her one of the heavy white masks that covered mouth and nose and made her feel stifled, suffocating.

It *was* chokingly dusty work, and Juliet hated every moment of it. Before long the air even in that vast room was clouded with a fine penetrating powder that permeated every nook and cranny and crevice. They hammered and banged and chiselled, filling sack after sack with rubble, piling any larger reusable bricks or stones to one side, to be sold or recycled within the house, whatever seemed best. Juliet could feel her stomach churn and knot with every piece that fell from the doorway, every increase of the opening. But Leo was in high spirits, even humming a rhythmic growling counterpoint to his work. Muffled by the mask though they were, Juliet recognised—just—some of the tunes he was attempting: old Rolling Stones songs, or Pink Floyd. Long ago, he used to sing them, loudly, while driving, especially when navigating some foreign road on one of their many holidays.

Luke would put his hands to his ears with an expression of exaggerated anguish. *'Oh Dad, please! Not the golden oldies!'* After which Leo would make some attempt at one of Luke's current favourites, though he'd have to tell Luke what it was, knowing his son had no hope of recognising it from his father's rendering. It would all end in laughter, happy, loving shared laughter, in which Juliet would join too. She could barely remember now what that had felt like, so far removed was it from this life without Luke. Even in the few moments these days when she'd come nearest to happiness it had been beyond recall, and this was not one of them. She could feel the tears rising in her throat, so she forced them back and attacked the rubble with renewed determination. Seconds later Leo suddenly stopped humming in mid-bar and fell silent. Had he too recalled those times, and found the memory more than he could bear? Perhaps he simply found the dust and heat of the mask too much for him. Whatever the reason, there was no more humming after that.

A few moments later, Leo gave a cry. 'Look! There! Perfect!' He was gazing into the hole that was growing by the minute in the infilled doorway.

Juliet did not want to look, but she forced herself forward, trying to breathe deeply to calm her thudding heart. A quick glance, and she glimpsed worn stone steps; that was more than enough. Her limbs were shaking. 'I need a coffee! Do you want one?' She began to retreat.

'Oh we must finish this now we've started! I couldn't bear to leave it like this, so near—We're just about ready for the prop. There's just these last few to be cleared.'

'I can't do any more without a drink.' She turned and ran.

Once out of the room, clear of the dust, mask off, she drew deep breaths, slowed her pace, began to feel a little better. In the kitchen, she made coffee—for Leo too—while Tiger twined himself about her ankles, a soft comforting presence. She drank all of her coffee before she braced herself to set out with Leo's mug back to the hall.

He greeted her with a frown, though he said nothing, gulped down the drink, then with a 'Right, now!' set to work on the remaining infill. 'Come on, do your bit!'

So she did, and then helped him manoeuvre the prop into place, though even she could see the doorway would have held without it. What she could also see, all too clearly, was the spiral stair, intact, complete, winding away from them towards the non-existent upper floor.

Leo took a torch from his bag of tools and stepped through the doorway.

'Don't!'

He turned to look at her. 'Why ever not?'

'It might collapse on you!'

He gave a derisive snort and continued on his way until he had disappeared from sight. She heard his feet on the steps, one, two, three, up and up. Her heart thudded: steps, like those others—no, for these sounded eager, brisk, sharper somehow. How many? Fifteen? Twenty?

They stopped: silence. What was happening? What had Leo found—or seen? A moment, an instant of rising panic—and then she heard him coming back down, more slowly, carefully…

He was in the doorway again, his face alight. 'They go right up to what would have been the first floor, just where those holes are that held the rafters. *And* there's another blocked doorway up there!' What he read in her expression she did not know, but it made him give a gentle laugh. 'Don't worry, I'm not suggesting we tackle that. Not yet anyway—we'd need a floor to walk out onto. One day maybe, but that really is something that will have to wait.' He stood back and gazed at their handiwork. 'I'll have to get a door for that. An antique one, in keeping. Take some doing—it's a good size.'

'More reclamation yards?' Juliet's voice was tremulous rather than teasing. She had been trying to control her shivering, but by now it was obvious even to Leo.

'You're cold. Shall we open a tin of soup for lunch?'

'I made some yesterday.'

He flung a satisfied arm about her. 'Then let's go and eat it shall we? I'm starving! I'll clear up afterwards. Put some polythene sheeting over the doorway too, keep the draughts down. A good morning's work, you must agree.'

A happy man, he followed her from the room. She wished she could as easily remove the inexplicably haunting image of that opened doorway from her mind.

The wind stirred the polythene, set it rattling. Through it a shadow came, flickered on the ancient arch of the door, wavered and crossed the threshold…

Alone in her bed, earplugs firmly in place, Juliet had still felt uneasy that night, and it had taken her some time to fall asleep; and then she dreamed.

Or did she? She knew she was asleep, yet she was acutely aware that she was lying in her bed, here in this room, listening.

Torchlight flickering in the night; banging, banging on the door, clamorous voices…

A fierce gust howled through the gap, setting the place alive with noise and movement.

A pause. The clatter of hooves on cobbles, dwindling to silence.

Slow feet mounting the stairs…darkness…

She heard them, the steps on the creaking boards beyond the bedroom door. The earplugs did nothing to screen out the sound.

The terror was real enough, but this time she was unable to move, could not reach out and switch on the bedside lamp. She could do nothing at all but lie frozen there, paralysed, as the steps reached her door; came to a halt…*'No…no!'* screamed a voice in her head, dragged from somewhere deep inside her. There followed what seemed an interminable moment of waiting that stretched out in silence, while she lay, open-eyed, hearing strained for the least sound, against all her instincts.

The door latch lifted, the door edged open. Something shadowy shivered into the room. The steps approached, nearing the bed. It was cold, very cold, but she was completely unable to move, to pull the duvet closer about her, could not even shut her eyes. She had to watch in impotent terror as the shape drew nearer and nearer, silently now, with no sound of steps, no creaking of boards.

Then, a moment of darkness, utter darkness, like the deepest sleep, except that a part of her mind still knew it was there, that it was not sleep…

She came slowly back to consciousness, aware first of a light, a gentle point of light close to the bed; a light that flickered and bent in the draught from the windows. A flame: a candle flame, from the candle that stood in a holder on the bedside table—not her familiar lamp, but a candle; and it was not after all a bedside table, but a stool. The flame cast a softening light on the rich purple shades of the bed hangings, so that it was only near at hand, on the curtain close to her head, that she could see how threadbare they were. It lit the carved chest just visible at the foot of the bed and the heavy ornate cupboard at the far side of the room, near the stone fireplace in which the embers of a fire still glowed. It lit the panelled walls, the bare floorboards, a glimpse of a crucifix hanging above a prayer desk on which a rosary lay…She was—who was she? The woman frozen on the bed? The woman who looked out on what was safe and familiar, or should have been? She recognised the shape of the room, its windows, but nothing else—yet she knew it was hers, all this was hers…

He has gone, my darling has gone. They've taken him from me, my son, my dear one. Torn from my arms, from my heart—no not from my heart, for he is there still, searing it with pain. Lord have mercy, Lord have mercy!

The world has gone dark, the moon snuffed out, the stars extinguished. But I must bear it, I must. It is God's will and I cannot make it otherwise, only trust, and hope—without hope. Trust and do my duty, day by day, day after long day…

It had not happened in this room, yet she could see it as if in memory, repeating in an endless loop in her mind. Downstairs, when he'd run to her in the doorway, she'd clutched the child to her, tried to escape with him up the stairs, but they'd come all the same, snatched him from her, lifted him onto the back of the horse, ridden away into the night—He'd struggled, shouted, screamed, but they were strong and he was slightly made.

So like Luke when he'd been that age…

Her head filled with noise, obliterating the scene. Darkness flooded in, a moment of utter bewilderment. Then panic.

*Luke! I must stop him—He mustn't drive that car—Leo, take it back, now, before it's too late! Don't even make the promise! I must wake up and stop it happening, make time go back and all will be well…*She was struggling, struggling to breathe, to open her eyes, to see.

She pulled out the earplugs, reached to switch on the light—her bedside light, with its pale silk shade. There it was, brightly illuminated, her own familiar room, the rug on the floor, all glowing colours, the pale painted walls, the Victorian wardrobe, the pile of packing cases, the soft green curtains filtering the moonlight. And the only sound the wind in the trees, that incessant sound that was becoming the background to their new lives. All was well.

Only it wasn't, for Luke was dead and nothing, ever, could bring him back. He had gone. Nothing she had done, nothing she had tried to do, nothing at all had been able to save him. Leo had bought the car; Luke had accepted it. She would never forget the look on his face when he saw it parked in front of the house, the utter disbelieving joy. For a moment —just a moment—she had forgotten her anxieties in the totality of his delight. He'd hugged them both.

Then he'd taken it for a spin, with Katie beside him. 'Don't worry, Mum! I'll be fine! I'm a great driver, aren't I, Dad—?'

And the next thing was the knock on the door, the two police officers, a man and a woman, standing there. 'Mrs Marston? You have a son, Luke?'

She'd known then, at that very moment, she'd known with every part of her, though she'd heard herself answer calmly enough, 'Yes, he's my son,' and at their grave, gentle, 'May we come in?' she'd let them in, through the hall, into the living room, with the squishy sofas and long windows that somehow would never afterwards look the same. Because nothing would ever look the same, nothing would ever *be* the same, could not be.

He had gone. The light and focus of her life, snuffed out in a moment. All those years, eighteen years, from the night when she'd given birth in the flower-filled hospital room, heard his first cry at the end of a long and arduous labour, and then held him in her arms, wrapped against the world, seen the soft fuzz of his baby hair, the tiny hands, the deep blue eyes opening to hers.

His eyes had turned brown, his hair mousy-fair, he had grown sturdy and bright, her son, her joy. There'd been no others. She'd been well into her thirties when he was born, after years of bitter disappointment. All those miscarriages, year after year, so that in the end they'd decided it was less painful simply to assume they'd always be childless, to give up trying. It was then, at the moment of acceptance, that she'd suddenly, unexpectedly, found herself pregnant again. And this time it had all gone as it should.

She had held him in her arms at last—their miracle baby, the longed-for infant, their hope for the future—

She felt the tears spring to her eyes, the sad slow soft tears that often came unbidden, unwanted; and brought no ease. He had gone.

It was the ordinariness of the kitchen that seemed unreal today, the cereal packets, the fridge humming away in the silence, the kitten sleeping in his basket; and Leo coming into the room. He helped himself to cornflakes and toast and joined her at the table, where she was sitting gazing at her muesli without really seeing it, the spoon shaking a little in her hand.

'What's the matter?'

She blinked, focussed her eyes on him. 'Nothing. Just thinking.'

He gave her a sharp suspicious look—it was clear that he knew something had disturbed her sleep, but had no intention of probing further. He'd made his view of such things clear and that was the end of it. 'I'm off to look for that door. Do you want to come?'

'No—no thank you.' She shuddered at the very thought of the doorway, closed or open.

She would have spent the morning in the garden, that place of healing, but it was pouring with rain. Trying to keep her mind on wholesome things, she sat at her desk and ordered a couple of gardening history books from Amazon—they might give her ideas as to how to recreate what had once been here. But even that could not distract her from the memories of the night, or stop her heart beating faster at every small sound.

In the end, on impulse, she picked up the phone and rang the rectory. 'Rosie? Will you be in if I come over?' She tried to sound cheerfully matter-of-fact, as if arranging an agreeable social visit, but she wasn't sure if she'd succeeded. In any case, if Rosalind was busy she might refuse a mere social call, where a matter of need would claim her attention. Would she simply remind Juliet that they'd already planned to meet the following Monday?

'Oh Juliet, I'm sorry—I'm just dashing out to take a service. All Saints today. Should be back by eleven thirty, if you want to come and have a coffee then—or lunch.'

She drove to Meadhope anyway, just to get out of the house, and slipped into a pew at the back of the church, letting the words of the service wash over her without actually participating. All those prayers about saints in days gone by, centuries of individuals, *'St Luke and all the saints…'*

Phrases snagged on the anguished barbs of her mind…*strangers and pilgrims here on earth…*A lady in black who walked in a garden…and at night wandered restlessly—? Or did she? Was it all pure imagination? Or was it an echo some long-dead inhabitant had left in the place, a shadow of what she had been? Were those echoes everywhere one went, yet mostly invisible, the traces of so many emotions, so much heartache and joy, left in the walls that had enclosed those long past lives? What had happened last night had seemed so much more substantial than that, so much more real, horribly real.

It was odd, hearing Rosalind's voice intoning the words, seeing her in her place in the chancel, with the eyes of her congregation on her. Juliet felt as if the Rosalind of their shared childhood had gone, to be replaced by a stranger, the woman priest performing the rites of her office. Her thoughts went back to the visit the other day. She'd taken Rosalind's assurances at face value, that she had come as a friend. Yet Juliet was a parishioner, and Rosalind a priest. Could she ever shrug off her pastoral role, and become again the old friend she had been? Especially when Juliet considered how their youthful friendship had ended. Wasn't it more likely that Rosalind the priest had put aside her own resentment, her sense of betrayal, pretended she did not even remember them, and come to her, not as an old friend, but as a priest calling on a parishioner who needed her support? Perhaps she even had some hope that Juliet would feel drawn to attend church Sunday by Sunday.

Juliet felt herself recoil at the thought of confiding in Rosalind today. If she were to do so, telling her—as best she could—about what had happened last night, she knew she would be wondering at every reaction if the woman listening was the friend or the priest, while always suspecting that she was simply the latter.

As soon as the service showed signs of ending she slipped out of the church, got back into the car and drove home. She had just put her car keys down on the dresser when her phone rang. It was Rosalind; she felt her heart sink. What should she say?

'Didn't I see you at the back of church? Are you coming round?'

'No, I'm OK thanks. Sorry to have bothered you.'

There was a little pause. 'Something's happened, hasn't it?'

'Oh, nothing important. I'm fine.'

She was trying to find the right formula to end the call, when Rosalind went on, 'I found out something interesting about your house the other day.'

Juliet felt her heart lurch. 'Oh? What was that?'

'There was a party at Ashburn Hall—near my other church, a tiny village, more a hamlet really.'

'I know of it.'

'We got talking to the birthday boy's sister, Caroline Stanway—'

Juliet murmured the name reflectively. 'Oh —wasn't there a horsewoman of that name? Really good, Olympic standard?'

'It's possible. They're certainly a horsey sort of family. I don't know much about her otherwise, except that she's married and lives somewhere in the Midlands—Leicestershire, I think. But it seems Ashburn Hall was one of several locally that were owned by Catholic families, at the time when Catholics were persecuted. She thought Holywell was another.' She hesitated a moment, then said, 'She did ask if you'd seen the ghost. Though when I pressed her about it, she laughed it off as something all old houses were supposed to have.'

Had Josh said something to his mother? Juliet forced a laugh. 'It would be a brave ghost that got past Tiger!'

'Tiger?'

'Oh, Leo's bought me a kitten. He's gorgeous.' And mention of him had given her an idea: she would take him upstairs with her tonight. 'I mustn't take any more of your time. I know how busy you are.'

'See you on Monday then. You haven't forgotten?'

'Absolutely not,' she said brightly. 'Looking forward to it.'

That afternoon, Rosalind finished her round of sick communions a little earlier than she had expected—one of her regulars had been taken to stay for a time with her daughter, but had forgotten to let Rosalind know. With unscheduled time on her hands, she followed the niggle of her conscience and went to see her mother-in-law, though there were many other things she could have been doing, simply to catch up.

She made her way to the back of the house and tapped on the door, waiting a little while for Jessie to come and open it. When nothing happened, she tried the handle, only to find the door locked, which was odd—Jessie usually left the back door unlocked during the day, if she was at home. Rosalind had a key to the house, but she was concerned not to take Jessie's privacy for granted. It was her home, and Rosalind was in a sense always a guest in it, especially when calling uninvited, as now.

When she'd knocked three times and there was still no reply, she let herself in. The kitchen was empty, but on the cooker stood a saucepan of peeled potatoes standing in water, as if ready to have the gas turned on under it. Jessie usually cooked a large midday meal, but by now it was well into the afternoon, long past lunch time. Had she decided to eat her main meal in the evening, in spite of her frequent assertions that a heavy meal late in the day played havoc with the digestion? It seemed unlikely. Anxiety twisted in Rosalind's stomach. 'Jessie!' she called, though not so loudly as to risk Jessie's usual rebuke: *'There's no need to shout!'*

Still no reply. She advanced into the hall, peeped into the lounge. Jessie sat by the unlit fire, apparently asleep. Perhaps—forgetting about the potatoes—she'd eaten something different for lunch and was now deep into her afternoon nap. Rosalind moved quietly forward. The old woman looked very frail, sitting there with her eyes closed, pale and gaunt. Rosalind felt a surge of compassion. However irritating her mother-in-law might be, it couldn't be much fun for her, growing older, increasingly dependent on others. She sat down on the end of the sofa nearest to her chair.

With a kind of snort Jessie woke suddenly. Her eyes looked mistily blue, taking some time before fixing on Rosalind with something less than their usual penetrating sharpness. 'What…? Who…? Oh, Rosalind!' With a visible effort, she forced herself to an upright position.

Had her words been just a little slurred? Rosalind wasn't sure, but something didn't feel quite normal, though not in any very obvious way. 'Are you all right, Jessie?'

'Of course.' Her crisp tones were exactly as they always had been, incisive, dismissive of any hint of weakness on anyone's part, her own included. 'Why shouldn't I be?' Then she added, 'Was I expecting you?'

That uncertainty was not like her at all. Now Rosalind knew for sure that something was not right, but all she said was, 'No, I'm afraid I've dropped in without warning—very inconsiderate of me. Shall I make us a cup of tea? Have you had your lunch?'

'I'm perfectly capable of making my own

luncheon.' Jessie pressed her hands on the arms of her chair as if to lever herself up, then evidently changed her mind and continued to sit where she was.

'Of course you are.' So she hadn't eaten yet! What had been going on? 'But wouldn't you like to be waited on for a change? I can make you something.'

'Perhaps a cup of tea.' Then, inevitably, as if Rosalind still needed a reminder after all these years: 'Weak, a little milk, no sugar.'

The remark had become a family catchphrase—at least when Jessie was not around to hear it—and Rosalind smiled to herself as she went to put the kettle on.

As they sat sipping their tea, Rosalind said gently, 'You should eat something, you know. Would you like to come back to the rectory with me? I've got some soup already made.'

'I prefer to eat properly at midday, as you know. Besides, you put too much spice in your food. You know how it disagrees with me. I have one of those ready meals Alastair brought me in the refrigerator. A roast beef dinner. That will do me nicely for today.'

'Then let me do it for you.'

She prepared the meal—the potatoes could wait until tomorrow—and brought it to Jessie on a tray, a little reassured to see how eagerly the old lady ate. Anxious to prolong her visit until she was fully easy in her mind about Jessie's state of health, Rosalind lingered to tell her a little about Josh's researches. 'He's become very interested in the history of an old house in the parish, Holywell. It's good to see him enjoying something again.'

Concern for the welfare of her grandson was something that Jessie could share with Rosalind. 'Yes, he needs an interest, after all that's happened. It was a distressing episode.'

Rosalind was doubtful if Josh would have liked to have his brief marriage and the death of his wife referred to as merely a distressing episode, but she said only, 'It's difficult because we never met her. It makes it harder to share what he's going through, as we would have done if we'd known Miriam.'

'It might have made it harder still if you had met her,' Jessie retorted.

Rosalind knew that the old lady had disapproved of the very idea of her grandson being involved with an African woman, but didn't want to become tangled in yet another fruitless discussion of the matter. She made some non-committal murmur, then said, 'He's been sitting up all night reading ancient local history books. He's talking about doing some research in Durham next.'

'Perhaps he will write about it afterwards.'

'That would be a great idea. Perhaps he will.' She glanced at the hearth. 'Would you like the fire on? It's beginning to feel a bit chilly.'

'I shall be going upstairs soon—that will warm me up. First I'll take this back to the kitchen.' She put the tray to one side and this time did lever herself out of the chair. As she did so, Rosalind caught sight of a purple-red mark on her wrist, where the cuff slid back.

'Oh, what did you do there?'

'Och, I caught it on something yesterday.' Jessie dismissed the matter with a wave of her hand. But as she began to walk across the room, Rosalind saw how she clung for support to the furniture much more than usual and how she avoided putting weight on her left leg for longer than the briefest of moments.

She went to her mother-in-law, took the tray from her and looped her arm through Jessie's, offering an additional support that was— disturbingly—accepted without a murmur. 'Come now, Jessie,' she urged gently. 'This was more than just catching yourself, wasn't it?'

'Just a wee tumble, that's all.' Adding with some asperity: 'I don't doubt even you have had the occasional tumble yourself, more than once in your life.'

'Of course I have.' She could hear how much Jessie was gasping for breath after so small an exertion, and suggested a rest on one of the dining chairs; that her offer was taken up was more alarming than ever. Rosalind sat down beside her. 'This is more than just an occasional tumble, isn't it?' She saw the obdurate look on Jessie's face, and took her hand, saying very gently, 'Jessie, we worry about you, you know. Why don't you have another think about that alarm? Just to reassure us all?'

'It's all right for you, so independent as you are. Please yourself and no one to deny you. Can you not leave me that little bit of freedom, not to be dependent on strangers? It's no fun growing old, you know.'

There was such a note of pathos in her voice that Rosalind was shaken by it. Jessie was not a woman who pleaded for anything, ever— commanded, yes, often, but as someone asking for what was her due, not pleading for understanding. There was resentment in her words too, at her daughter-in-law's freedom, which was nothing new, for she had often made it clear that she disapproved of what she saw as Rosalind's unfeminine pursuit of a career, while she apparently discounted completely the vocational and spiritual elements of her calling. But now—had there been something else in her tone, something that was almost envy? Could it be that some of Jessie's animosity was for the woman who—unlike her traditional stay-at-home mother-in-law—had an important role in the community, an absorbing calling? And now Jessie, after a lifetime of caring for husband and son, of being in some measure subservient to each of them, had nothing left, not even her own small measure of independence.

Rosalind, filled with real compassion, stroked her hand. 'But wouldn't it free you, to know you didn't have to worry about the possibility of having a fall, to know that whatever happened there would be someone you could call on—for instance, if we happened to be out for the day, or away on holiday? It would leave you able to get on with your life without worry.'

She could see that she'd touched some chord in Jessie, that this was indeed something that clouded her life. But even before the old woman replied Rosalind saw how she still recoiled from admitting her need.

'It would worry me more to know I might be putting a complete stranger to such trouble.'

She gathered all her strength and rose to her feet again. 'Now, I shall go and wash up. I expect you have things you must be getting on with too.'

It was a clear dismissal, so Rosalind could only kiss her and go.

'Your mother's had another fall,' Rosalind told Alastair later, over supper. It was just the two of them tonight, as Josh had—unusually, and to his parents' gratification—gone to meet an old school friend. 'I wonder if there's a bit more to it than that—more than just losing her balance, I mean. She just didn't seem herself, not at first, though by the time I left she was fine.' And exactly as she always had been, even to the astringency of her manner, thought Rosalind ruefully. 'I tried mentioning the alarm again, with the usual result.' She took a bite of the onion bread Alastair had brought home with him to go with the hearty vegetable stew he'd prepared at the weekend. 'I do wonder if she might give it more consideration if she had something to do to give her a sense of purpose.'

'You mean more than just keeping us running round after her? But she has her garden, she reads a good deal, she knits and sews.'

'I don't think that's enough. She wants to be needed.'

'Don't we all?' he observed with a grin.

Rosalind did not smile. 'Yes. Precisely.'

He studied her grave face. 'Hmm. Yes. I see what you mean. The trouble is, to be useful to people you need to have something to give. Other than carping and criticism, that is. Just imagine if, say, you got her to befriend some lonely old soul in the parish. She'd hardly bring sunshine into their lives, would she?'

'Hardly. Though of course there are lots of old people who love nothing better than a good grumble. What we need is to find a kindred spirit, someone who's lost without a companion in misery!'

'Pity Nurse Hutchinson's such a positive person, for all her abrasiveness.' Meadhope's long-retired midwife, whom few dared to address by her Christian name, was a fiercely independent woman of forthright views. She'd always been a good neighbour to Jessie, who liked her as much because she was a fellow Scot as for anything else, but she could not be said to be a grumbler, nor had she much patience with those who did grumble. 'The sad thing is that, for all her kindness, I don't think she really likes my mother very much.'

No surprise there, thought Rosalind, though she said nothing.

Juliet fell asleep quickly that night, earplugs in and Tiger curled up, a warm lightweight, on her feet. It was a long time since she had slept so soundly, so quietly, without dreams or disturbance.

She had no idea what time it was when a sudden chill roused her, though it was very dark. The kitten's comforting warmth had gone. 'Tiger!'

In spite of the earplugs, she heard a mew from somewhere near the door. 'Oh, you don't want to go out, do you? You've got a litter tray in here, you know—I showed it to you. Silly cat!'

Another mew; and then a sudden anguished yowl. She switched on the light.

The kitten stood facing the door, its fur bristling along the arch of its back. It spat, yowled again, retreated backwards towards the bed. There it leapt up and dived under the duvet, yowling still.

Juliet shivered, clutching the animal to her, stroking the ruffled fur. 'It's all right! It's all right!'

But it wasn't all right. Something had

terrified the kitten, something that this time Juliet herself could not hear or feel or see.

She pulled the duvet over them both and cowered there, holding the kitten close. She did not sleep again that night.

Chapter Nine

The café was packed when they reached it
the following Monday, but someone was just
leaving a table in a far corner, which offered
Rosalind and Juliet a measure of privacy. They
waited while a young waitress cleared and
wiped down the table, then brought copies of
the menu.

'A day for naughty treats, I think,' Juliet
declared. 'Or is that not something a vicar
allows herself?'

'Oh, now and then. Certainly today!'

'Do you find it hard, having to be a vicar all
the time? Do you have to watch your step every
moment of the day?'

'No—well, not really. But I suppose I'm
more conscious than many people of the ethical
dimension to everything one does. Or I ought to
be anyway.'

'So you don't worry about money or
concern yourself with investments and things?'

'Oh, I'd be as worried as the next man or
woman if all my savings were tied up in some
dodgy financial institution. I can certainly
sympathise with people who are in that position.
Like anyone else, even vicars have to make
sensible provision for the future. But it's more a

case of not being obsessed with money, of never making it the first consideration, never choosing to do something simply because it's financially rewarding. If I ever felt called to a course of action that meant living in poverty, then so be it.'

'But what about your husband? And if you had dependent children?'

'That makes it more complicated. I suppose that's the logic of the Roman Catholic position on celibate priests. On the other hand, if someone's married a priest, then they know what to expect—it's part of the deal. But I wasn't a priest when Alastair and I got married, so it was more a case of him understanding each step of the way what was involved, what I was asking of him.'

'Is he OK with that?'

'There have been moments…but yes, he's always been really supportive. Of course, the fact that he has a reasonably well paid job helps. He pays our mortgage.'

'Oh, so you won't be out on the street when you retire? When do you retire, by the way?'

'Seventy is the compulsory retirement age.'

Juliet whistled. 'That's tough!'

'We can go before—and I guess I will. But believe me there are a good few priests who'd go on for ever if they had the chance—often to the despair of their parishioners.'

'So you have a house then? You don't own the rectory, do you?'

'It goes with the job. But we have a cottage in Swaledale. We used to use it for holidays, but now it's on a long let to a local couple who couldn't afford anywhere to buy in the area—ironically, I suppose, because so many of the houses are bought up as second homes. Like ours. Though at least it's the only house we actually own.'

'Will you live there when you retire?'

'Who knows? It's more of a safety net than anything.' She smiled. 'I certainly wouldn't want to be doing up a ruin as you're doing! I think it's very brave of you.'

'Brave being code for insane, as I recall! I suppose we are. Certainly it feels like it just at the moment. Though Leo believes he got out of the City just in time. He's said for a long time that it was a lot more precarious than it looked, that there was a lot of dodgy stuff going on. So maybe we've done the sane thing after all. But if things don't work out with the house I guess we'd find it hard to sell and we'd have most of our money tied up in it and nowhere to go. So it has to work. No matter what.'

Rosalind studied her face. 'Something did happen last week, didn't it? All Saints' Day, Thursday, when you phoned me.'

Juliet shrugged. 'Something and nothing… Do you think that waitress is ever going to come and take our order?' She looked round and gestured to the girl, who came over, smiling, notebook in hand. 'I'll have the soup, and a brie and bacon panini.'

'I'll have soup too—brown bread bun, please. And a Greek salad. And a glass of tap water.'

'A glass of white wine for me, please.' She glanced at Rosalind. 'I'm not driving home until late—I'm meeting Katie at the station at five-ish.'

'Oh! The girl who was your son's girlfriend?'

'That's right. I'm so looking forward to it.'

'I'd like to meet her. How long is she staying?'

'I'm not sure—I didn't ask. I was just so pleased she was coming. I hope it'll be a good long time. But she does have a job to go back to, so I don't know. We've had the odd phone call, but we haven't met since—well, when we scattered Luke's ashes…' She gazed across the table at Rosalind's attentive face and abruptly forgot all her misgivings about her old friend's motives, her doubt that the renewed friendship was real. She was conscious only that there were things she had long needed to say, if only she'd had someone to confide in—as now she had. 'It was Katie's idea. They'd had a holiday together in Cornwall, just a few weeks before. They went surfing, all that. Luke loved it. Katie said he'd stood on the beach one evening gazing out to sea and said, 'When I die, I want my ashes scattered here.' So that's what we did.' Her eyes brimmed with tears. 'I would have liked a grave, a place to visit, where I could put flowers, and remember, but...' She swallowed hard. 'There we are. It was what he wanted.' Taking a tissue from her handbag, she blew her nose. 'Sometimes I'm afraid Katie will disappear from our lives. We look on her as our daughter-in-law, but of course she isn't. She's just the girl Luke loved. So—well, I'm thankful she asked to come.' Then she smiled. 'But it's silly really. How could anyone who'd loved Luke ever give a thought to anyone else?'

Rosalind thought that was a perilous assumption. Looking back, she recalled the people her own children had been with (or aspired to be with) while in the sixth form at school. They might have believed they were deeply in love, but none of those early relationships had survived for very long, especially once they left home for university. But she could hardly say so to Juliet, facing her across the table with those tears of heartache in her eyes. She wondered what this clinging painful affection did to the girlfriend—or was she too held frozen in that time of teenage passion?

The drinks came, and then the soup—tomato and basil—and they ate in silence for a while; until Juliet said abruptly, 'Rosie, do you believe in ghosts?' She tried to make the question sound casual, but failed completely, though Rosalind appeared to take it at face value.

'Oh, now there's a tricky one! I don't disbelieve. I think there's obviously something people give that name to. Sometimes it's imagination or delusion, but not always, I think. But what it is, I don't know. A memory left in a place, a time overlap? The mark left by some joy or sorrow so great that it's scoured itself into the fabric of a place, just as something heavy dropped on a floor can mark the floorboards? I just don't know.'

'Evil spirits?'

'I rather doubt that, but I don't know—unless by evil spirits you mean the stain left by a wrong done to someone long ago, or by their pain and sorrow. Maybe we will know some day and there'll be a perfectly reasonable scientific explanation, but for now—well, it's a mystery.' She studied Juliet's face. 'You're not just asking out of casual interest are you? Something's happened at Holywell.'

'Has Josh said anything?'

'He said he'd heard sounds. Sobbing. And—that you had too.'

'There's been more, since…' Her voice dropped to a whisper. 'That night, before I phoned—Rosie, it's almost as if I'd been, well, possessed, as if someone came and took me over in my sleep. I was that other person, that woman.'

'How horrible!'

'It was; truly horrible—most of all because I felt her grief. It was so real, even to the room, and the furniture, nothing like what's there now. And then it got all mixed up with my own feelings about Luke. I wish I knew what was happening. It frightens me. Leo thinks I'm imagining it. I haven't even told him about this last thing. He'd just say I'd had a nightmare. He doesn't know Josh heard anything either. I wasn't sure how he'd react.' She smiled wanly. 'Silly really—that might make him believe me, if he knew it wasn't just me.'

'I don't think scepticism is any more logical than the apparently irrational. I'd guess nothing short of an earthquake is going to make him believe. And even that he'd probably put down to his overheated imagination.'

'Yes, I guess you're right. But what can I do, Rosie? It's getting so I'm scared to go to bed, or to be alone in the house. I took Tiger up with me Saturday night, and last night.'

'Did that help?'

'It made it worse, if anything. He was really spooked by something, in the middle of the night.'

Rosalind shivered, studying her friend's troubled face. 'Do you wish you'd stayed in London?'

Juliet considered the matter, trying to see her own feelings clearly. 'No.' She sounded surprised, as if her reply was unexpected even to herself. 'No, I don't. Somehow it feels more like something to be solved and put right, not something to run away from. But I don't know how to do it. And I'm frightened that if I don't it will all get much worse.' She smiled suddenly. 'You know, I didn't realise that was what I felt. There's one thing—the one place I feel happy is in the garden. That feels so right, trying to restore it to what it was once—or what I believe it was once. Does that sound ridiculous? It is really—I do my gardening when Leo's not around, in secret. He thinks I'm mad even thinking about it. I was never interested in gardening, you see. We were going to get someone in to do it for us, when we'd got the house right. And since he knows it was a dream started all this, and the scent of a rose that wasn't there—well, it does all seem a bit insane, doesn't it?'

'Perhaps. Yet gardening's such a wholesome and healing thing.' She poured coffee for them both. 'Perhaps when Josh has finished his research, if he manages to find out about this lady in your dream—perhaps then, when you understand, it'll all calm down.'

Juliet seized on the suggestion. 'Yes—yes, I'm sure you're right. Let's hope he gets to the bottom of it soon.' She took a deep breath. 'This is all getting too heavy for me! Tell me, do you know of anywhere good for an evening meal in the Meadhope area? We've found nothing so far.'

'There's a little place off a side road a few miles up the dale, an old country pub, a bit eccentric, but it does very good home-cooked food—nothing fancy, just good. Excellent

Sunday lunches, though you need to book. Here, I'll write down the details—' She wrote the name and telephone number on a paper napkin and passed it to Juliet.

'Sounds ideal. Thanks.' She saw suddenly that Rosalind's attention was no longer on her, her gaze fixed instead on some point at the far side of the cafe. She turned to look, and saw that she appeared to be watching a solid middle-aged man sitting at a table with a woman whose plain good-humoured face was full of affectionate laughter.

Rosalind grinned. 'Sorry—I just spotted someone.' She lowered her voice. 'See that couple over there. He's Jeremy from Ashburn Hall. And she's the woman I saw at his party— his mother said she was a gatecrasher.'

'Then I'd say he encouraged the crashing. Look at the way he's devouring her with his eyes. I think the roof could fall in and he wouldn't notice, not while she's there.'

'I sense a romance that hasn't got Mummy's approval,' said Rosalind. 'We got the distinct impression that the guests at his party were all chosen by his mother. He looked very lost— except when talking to that woman. Poor Jeremy!'

'One day he'll come back as a ghost,

wandering the hall, wringing his hands for his lost love, for what might-have-been.'

Rosalind giggled, relieved that Juliet could joke about such things. 'Maybe that's all your ghost is, someone thwarted in love.'

'Maybe.' Juliet's expression shadowed again. 'But it doesn't sound like anything so trivial as that. Or feel like it.'

'Is it that trivial, to love someone hopelessly, in the face of strong maternal disapproval? I suppose it is, compared to some things.' *Like losing a child…*

After lunch, they paid and left the cafe without Jeremy having noticed them, and then made their way up to the cathedral, where Rosalind knelt to say a prayer, as she always did when passing that way, and Juliet lit a candle and sat gazing at its gentle flame until it had faded almost to nothing.

'I don't know what lighting candles does exactly,' she said afterwards. 'But it feels good. Calming. As if you were doing something to help, to make a difference.' Yet as she had watched the flame she had thought of the candlelight she had woken to that night, the alien light from an age long past…

It was hard to walk along streets busy with students returning from lectures, meeting and greeting one another—as Luke would have done. He should have been embarking on his second year by now, a part of the place as these young people were. Juliet grew very quiet as they walked along the narrow cobbled streets and then down steep steps to the river bank.

'What are you thinking?' Rosalind asked after a while.

'All those precious young lives. And they're so careless of life, they just don't know how precious it is. They won't know until they're old and there's so little of it left. Or until they lose someone they love…I find that so sad—no, I find it terrifying.' A group of young men in muddied sports gear passed them, laughing, their voices loud in the clear frosty air. 'Sometimes, when I see them like that, I want to shake them, shout at them: don't take life so lightly! Don't break the hearts of those who love you! Of course, they'd just think I was mad.' She halted abruptly and stood looking over the fast flowing water. 'I just wish there was some way of making something good come out of all this. I thought the house might do it, but I'm beginning to think it's not enough.'

Rosalind stood beside her. 'What would you like to come from it?'

'For no more boys to drive like idiots. For no

more mothers to go through this anguish. Pie in the sky, isn't it? You can't change human nature.'

'I suppose if young drivers had a longer probationary period—or the driving test was more stringent in some way…'

'Perhaps they should show lurid films of accidents, before the test. But then when they see all these things in computer games, death isn't real, however gruesome it looks. Besides, every boy thinks he's invincible—and that he's a wonderful driver however fast he drives.' She gave a resigned shake of the head. 'It's no good, is it? Sometimes I think life's too hard to go on —' She gazed at the water as if tempted even at that moment to throw herself into it.

Rosalind took her by the elbow, steering her gently back onto the path. 'Suicide leaves as much havoc and heartache behind as an accident does, believe me.'

'But who have I got left to care what becomes of me?'

'Leo. You know that. Maybe he's unfinished business—you both have unfinished business to sort out.'

'Yes.' She gave a sudden wintry smile. 'And that lady to pin down. If Josh can find out who she is—who she was.'

* * *

'Well, I see you've got a firework display in my honour,' said Katie, as Juliet embraced her on the platform at Durham station. In all directions over the city blooms of light rose, spread, scattered in the night sky, blue and green and gold, red and silver.

'I'm afraid it's all you'll get this Bonfire night,' Juliet said, leading the way to the car park. 'We haven't got anything special laid on.'

'I'm not missing a thing. I've been watching them from the train all the way up. One display after another. It's been great.' After a pause while Juliet negotiated a busy set of traffic lights, she asked, 'How are you both? How's the new house?'

'Exciting. A lot of work to be done…And you?'

No mention yet of Luke, Katie thought. How long before he came into the conversation? 'Oh, I'm fine. Work's going well. I enjoy it.'

'But surely not as a permanent career?'

'Probably not. I don't know yet. It's early days.'

'You're such a gifted person. I don't think Luke would have wanted you to give up all your hopes and ambitions because of what happened to him.'

'Oh, it wouldn't—' Kate stopped abruptly. She couldn't say, as she had been about to do, that what Luke might have thought was irrelevant to her now. She fell silent while she tried to find an acceptable response. 'It's taken such a long time to get my health back. I don't want to rush things. When I decide what to do it's got to be the right thing.'

'Of course. But how are you now? You're certainly looking very well.'

'If you don't count all the bits of metal in my body, I'm about back to normal. As normal as anyone can be, that is.'

'I'm glad. And very glad you still find time for us.'

'I'll always do that.'

Katie had not known quite what to expect, but she was enchanted with Holywell, even in the dark when most of its splendour was hidden. 'Oh, I can see why you fell in love with it!'

Juliet showed her to the only guest room that was fit for occupation. It looked over the garden, a calm pale-green-washed room of elegant eighteenth century proportions, its bed covered in antique lace, the empty fireplace shielded by an embroidered firescreen picked up in a local auction room. Juliet had designed the room with care, and with Katie in mind, as their most longed-for guest. 'No ensuite yet, I'm afraid. But the bathroom's just next door.' She went to close the curtains, as it was too dark to see anything outside.

'It's lovely!' Katie looked about her, taking it all in—'Oh!' On the Victorian washstand near the window stood a photograph of Luke, taken in the garden at Chelsea in all his carefree youth.

'You don't mind? It's not too painful having that there?'

'No, of course not! I'm very glad.' So young he looked, his face untouched by any marks of experience, untouched by care—Not like hers, glimpsed in the nearby mirror, with the tiny lines etched by weeks of pain, by the struggle to rebuild her life, by everything that had happened to her since that April day. Not two years ago, yet it felt as remote as the time when this room had been new.

'I'll leave you to get settled in, then we'll have supper—if I can drag Leo from his hammering!'

As Juliet left the room, Katie felt herself relax, let go of the tension. This wasn't going to be easy—but then she hadn't expected it to be. It was just something that had to be done.

Chapter Ten

The knocking startled Tiger, who set off in a dance around the room, leaping and tumbling after his tail and almost tripping Juliet up as she made her way to open the door.

'Josh! I didn't know you were coming!' She scooped up the wriggling kitten. 'How did you get here?'

'Fancied a walk—Is this a bad time?'

'Not at all. We've just been sitting around chatting since lunch—a really lazy afternoon. Come on in. To what do we owe the honour today?'

'I wanted to update you on progress so far.'

'Sounds promising.' She stood aside to let him in.

At the kitchen table, holding a mug of coffee, was a girl he'd never seen before. She moved as if to stand up and then clearly thought better of it and simply smiled at him.

'This is Katie,' Juliet said. 'Her first visit to Holywell.' She caught Josh's questioning look, and added in a low voice, 'Luke's girlfriend.'

The girl who'd been badly injured, Josh remembered, though she looked healthy enough. Slight, with glossy fair hair and blue eyes, she had the sleek well-groomed appearance that spoke of money and privilege. He greeted her warily. 'Hi!'

'I've been telling Katie about the research you're doing.'

How much else had Juliet told her? Why he was doing the research? About the noises, the dreams? He could see no indication of the answer on Katie's face, apart from a mild interest.

Juliet poured him coffee and he leaned back against the kitchen dresser, the mug cradled in his hands. 'I've done some costume research. I think she's definitely late sixteenth, early seventeenth century, our lady. Which narrows it down a bit. Also, it looks as if the people who lived here round that time may have been Catholics, when it was against the law to be anything but Church of England, but I couldn't find any names or anything. So I'm going to the University Library tomorrow to see if I can find out a bit more.'

Katie's clear tones broke in: 'Will you be disappointed if you find it was just a dream after all and the only person living here then was some fat farmer?'

If Juliet had told Katie the whole story she would surely never have spoken so lightly about it—and she would have known it was more than just a dream that he was investigating. 'Oh, very disappointed!' he said, matching her casual tone. Then: 'When did you get here?'

'Monday.' Had she heard any sounds during the two nights since then? Fresh-faced, rosy cheeked, she didn't look as if anything had troubled her unduly or disturbed her sleep. She smiled at Juliet, a warm sweet smile, quite unlike the polite good-mannered-girl's smile she had directed at Josh. 'It's a lovely place, this. A real haven.'

No, that settled it; she had definitely heard nothing.

'I said I'd take some coffee up to Leo,' said Juliet. 'He's grouting the tiles in what will eventually be our ensuite. Talk among yourselves!'

There was an awkward silence when she'd gone, which Katie broke at last: 'She's such a good person, Juliet. She's been very kind to me, they both have. They could have blamed me, but they didn't, not at all.'

'Blamed you for what?'

'You know I was in the car when Luke was killed? Their son? You do know all about that?'

'Yes—yes, Juliet told me. But it wasn't your fault.'

'They may have thought I'd encouraged him

to drive too fast. Or that he showed off more than he would have done otherwise because I was there, which I guess is possible—I just don't remember. Or there's the fact that I'm alive and he's not. Such a random thing.'

Some instinct made him ask, 'Do you feel bad about that?'

'Yes, sometimes. It used to be worse. At first I didn't even want to see Juliet and Leo, for fear of what they must be thinking. They were the ones who insisted, who made me feel they wanted to see me.'

'I suppose they're glad to have someone to talk to who remembers him. It's very hard when everyone else seems to have forgotten, and you know you never will. You want to talk and talk about the person you've lost, but no one else does. It's kind of bad manners.'

She studied him thoughtfully. 'You said that with real feeling.'

'Yes.' Then, as she said nothing, simply continued to gaze at him with gently questioning eyes: 'She died fourteen months ago. In Africa—Lesotho—of an AIDS-related illness. No one round here ever met her, not even my parents.'

'That must be very hard.'

'Don't get me wrong. My parents have been

wonderful. They encourage me to talk about her—their way of getting to know her, my Mum says. I just wish there was someone to share memories, not just listen to them.'

'You didn't want to stay in Lesotho then, where there'd be other people who knew her?'

'I got ill, after she died.' He glimpsed something that briefly showed in her expression. Recognising it for what it was, he said quickly, 'No, I haven't got AIDS—I had all the tests. It was some nasty tropical bug, but I'm fine now. But I couldn't stay and be a burden on everyone.'

'Will you ever go back?'

'I don't know. There's no one much out there either, not any longer, not who knew Miriam. But in the long run—who knows? I've started to get involved with the link Durham diocese has with Lesotho. Otherwise, I'm just taking one day at a time.'

'It's all you can do, isn't it? Look ahead any further and it's too bleak for words. To begin with at least—'

Juliet's return interrupted them. Josh took a last gulp of his coffee, then said to their host, 'I thought you might like to come along tomorrow, to the library.'

'Oh, I think I've enough to be getting on

with here. Besides, while Katie's with us—' She gestured towards her guest.

'Oh, but *I'd* love to come with you!' Katie broke in. 'Two heads are better than one and all that.'

Josh hesitated. Was that what he wanted, especially as she didn't know the whole story? Could he share the research with someone from whom he had to keep the truth? Besides—glancing at Juliet, he could see that she wasn't at all happy about it. That was hardly surprising; Katie had only just arrived, and her visit clearly meant a great deal to her hosts. Katie must have seen it too, for she said, 'You don't mind, do you, Juliet?'

'Of course not,' said Juliet, in a tone that completely belied her words.

'Do come along too!' the girl urged. 'Three heads are even better than two.'

This is getting out of hand, Josh thought with a sinking heart; just as Juliet said, 'Oh, sitting for hours in dusty libraries isn't my thing! Besides, we're due a visit from the English Heritage man —I need to be here for that. But you go. You'll enjoy it. You can tell me all about it over supper.'

The following morning, Katie and Josh set

out for Durham on the meandering local bus. As they were the only passengers, apart from a morose-looking old man far away at the front, Katie ventured to ask, 'Is something going on I don't know about?'

Josh gave her a sharp look. 'What do you mean?'

'Juliet, this morning: she looked as if she hadn't slept a wink, and she was pale as anything. I thought she looked tired the moment I arrived. I'm not sure, but I wonder if she even went to bed at all last night. I thought I heard her come upstairs just as it was starting to get light, though I could be wrong about that— maybe she'd just been to get a drink or something. But then this morning I overheard Leo talking to her, telling her to pull herself together and it was all her imagination and so on. I didn't think much about it—she never has slept all that well, since…well! But then later over breakfast I teased them about it being just the sort of house to have a headless ghost, and instead of laughing or making a joke of it they both gave me a very strange look and changed the subject.'

'What did Juliet tell you about this lady we're researching?'

'That she'd dreamed she saw her in the

garden and was convinced she was someone who'd once lived in the house. Sounds weird to me, but still. You seem to buy into it. Or are you just looking for something to do?'

'A bit of that, I suppose. Life's a bit dreary.' Should he tell her more, tell her the whole story, as far as he knew it? Or would that terrify her so much that she'd take the next train back to London?

He was still wondering what to do when she said, 'There is more to it than that isn't there?' Her eyes lit up. '*Is* the house haunted?'

'Juliet's heard things. And—so have I, one day when I was working there on Leo's computer. Footsteps, when there was no one there, and someone sobbing, really heartbreaking sobbing.'

She gave a dramatic shudder. 'Ugh! Scary stuff! And you think it was the woman in the dream?'

'I've no idea. But I thought it was worth looking into it, to see if I could find out anything. There might be something to explain it all.'

'That's a bit of a long shot.'

'Gives me something to do though, as you say.' Then he added, 'The funny thing is, I feel that's why I heard her. Because she wants someone to do something, to help somehow.'

'And you think this will?'

'I don't know. We'll have to wait and see won't we?' He laughed. 'All right, it *is* weird. But so what?'

They spent the day working steadily and carefully through heavy leather-bound volumes in which Victorian antiquarians had recorded the results of years of research—interminable results, expressed in the most dry and long-winded prose style. None of the books seemed to have anything remotely to do with Holywell.

After a fruitless morning, they abandoned the library for sandwiches and coffee in a nearby café, before returning, rather dejected by now, to the dusty volumes. It was towards the evening—and the library's closing time—when Katie gave a sudden exclamation. 'At last!' Then she dropped her voice to a whisper and slid the book she was reading along the table towards Josh. 'Look, there!' She indicated a paragraph on the right-hand page.

Holywell Manor near Meadhope was at that date the home of a lesser Recusant offshoot of the Machyns of Haroby Court in Warwickshire, who as owners of great estates in the Midlands were to come to prominence during the Civil Wars. It is reputed that this County Durham branch of the family had some minor involvement with the Gunpowder Plot.

'The Gunpowder Plot: that was—when? 1605 wasn't it? There was some sort of anniversary not long ago, I'm sure: the year before last…Funny to think I arrived here on Bonfire Night.' She saw at once from his expression that Josh had not grasped the connection, so explained it to him.

'Get you—quite the historian!' Perhaps Katie was going to be an asset after all. 'And that would fit with the costume Juliet drew.' He took it from his file and they studied it. Suddenly the woman in the drawing began to emerge from the rough sketch, not as a vague idea, but as a real person, with a place in history, perhaps even a tragic personal story. 'It doesn't prove anything, but I have a feeling we're on to something at last!'

'We need to find out more about this Machyn family. Where their great estates were, for instance. Perhaps there's a stately home we can visit. Do you think Haroby Court still exists? There could even be some members of the family left who know something about their history.'

'Come back to my place and we'll get on line!'

'No, better not—I promised I'd be back for

supper. But Juliet always cooks industrial quantities—I'm sure there'll be enough for you. Then we can use Juliet's computer, or Leo's.'

Haroby Court *did* still exist, and according to its website was opened to the public by its unnamed private owners at irregular periods during the summer. As it was now November, it was currently closed until the spring. 'Then we'll just have to contact them and ask if they know anything,' declared Katie.

'There's no email address.'

'So? It'll just have to be snail-mail, with a stamped addressed envelope. I'm good at letter writing. I'll compose something and email you a copy.'

'We could wait for ever for a reply. What if they're in the Caribbean for the winter?'

'If we don't try we shan't know. Don't be such a faint heart!'

Chapter Eleven

'I find myself wondering why she came at all if the first thing she does is go off for days on end,' grumbled Juliet. She and Leo were fitting plasterboard to the rough stone walls of the dining room, ready for replastering.

'She's doing it in the name of this research you're so interested in.'

'Aren't *you* interested in the history of this place?'

'Up to a point. I'm more interested in its future. Though what the English Heritage man had to say was interesting. He certainly knew his stuff. Wasn't he excited about the spiral stair?' He glanced at Juliet, who clearly wasn't sharing his enthusiasm. 'Katie's young. You can't expect her to want to hang around two old folks like us day after day.'

'We're her only link with Luke.'

He gazed at her, and she thought he was about to make some comment, but he must have thought better of it, for all he said was, 'True.' Then: 'It's only for one night, a couple of days.'

She said nothing. There was no point in saying she felt safer with Katie in the house, even though her presence had not made the sounds cease.

That night, as so often lately, she delayed going to bed for as long as she could bear, lingering on the sofa by the fire, the kitten asleep on her knee. Leo found her there when he came to tell her he was going upstairs; he never did so much before midnight. 'I thought you'd be in bed by now. Are you going to make a habit of staying up half the night?'

'What's it to you?'

'You're wearing yourself out. I do care about you, you know.'

In her exhausted state she found it hard to prevent the tears from filling her eyes. 'If you cared you'd take me seriously when—' She broke off. 'I'll come up soon. Good night.'

He shrugged and left her. Weary though she was, she made no move to follow him, but stayed where she was, pulling a throw over her for warmth, until at last she drifted into sleep.

Just as she'd feared, they came, in the dark, in the night, horses' hooves thudding, nearer, ever nearer. She had barred all the doors, warned the servants not to open to anyone, not even to the men who clattered to a halt in the yard and hammered on the door with cries of 'Open in the name of the law!'

Hammered and hammered, cudgels thudding on the wood, the rhythmic purposeful 'boom—boom' of something used as a battering ram…the din thundered in her brain, shuddered through her body.

There came a sudden crashing splintering sound; she felt a rush of air as the door swung wide. Armed men fell through it, shadows reaching into the house, elongated in the flickering rushlight, an army of grasping shadows, clutching at her happiness, seizing the heart from her.

She grasped her child and ran through the rooms, across the hall, up the stairs, seeking safety…

Too late: they followed her up the stairs, caught her from behind, sending her toppling, and seized him, right there in her arms, dragged him from her, down the stairs, through the door…They'd taken him and ridden away into the night, away from her, for ever.

She stood alone in the dark at the foot of the stairs and began to weep, anguished sobs wrenched from her very soul. She felt the stone of the walls rough and cold beneath her hand, the solid walls of this place she loved, a haven no longer…

Juliet jolted awake, her gaze adjusting to the dawn-lit room, trying to recall what she was doing here, how she had come to spend the night lying on the sofa. She remembered then: she had put off going to bed for fear of what awaited her there. Only now she knew with a shivering terror that even far from her bedroom there was no escape from the thing that had come to possess her.

It had seemed too good to be true: a guest house in Leamington Spa called *Haroby Court*, offering bed and breakfast for thirty pounds a night, with no single supplement, so Josh and Katie had checked into it, once they'd picked up the hire car on their arrival at the station.

Unfortunately, it *was* too good to be true. The *Haroby Court Guest House*, run down and smelling of damp, was owned by a harassed-looking woman whose obvious money worries only intensified the aura of hopelessness that hung over the place. Faced with a 'continental breakfast' so irredeemably awful that it reduced them to helpless giggles, they consumed enough of the flabby cornflakes, UHT milk and cold toast to keep them from fainting with hunger and found a greasy spoon café round the corner, where they devoured a full English breakfast, washed down by industrial strength tea.

'I'm really sorry!' Katie had found the guest house on line. 'It seemed fated. How wrong can you be?'

'Oh, I'd have done the same! At least it's cheap.'

'Not if you add in the extra fiver or so for this—' Katie indicated the fast disappearing food on her plate.

'Worth every penny.' Josh spoke through a mouthful of very good sausage. 'We won't need lunch after this. I feel ready for anything!'

The Savage family who owned Haroby Court—the real Haroby Court—had indeed been away from home when Katie's letter reached it, but their eventual emailed reply had been encouraging. Their ancestors, having made their money from judicious investments in railways and canals, had bought the property in the early nineteenth century, so had no connection with the Machyns, who had died out around the same time. However, there were a few items in the house that had once belonged to that family, along with a number of papers that were now in the County Record Office near Warwick. They were welcome to visit Haroby Court at a mutually convenient time, the letter said, where the housekeeper Mrs Ann Westbury would be glad to show them around.

So here they were, looking forward to a day of exploration. A fine classical mansion lay before them. 'Wrong period altogether,' said Katie knowledgeably. 'Looks eighteenth century.'

As indeed it was, so Mrs Westbury confirmed. 'It was completely rebuilt by the last of the Machyns in the late eighteenth century. He got himself so up to the neck in debt as a result that he shot himself. Which is how it came into the hands of the current owner's family.

Being rather more frugally minded, the Savages retained many of the fine things that their predecessors had left, as you will see.'

By the end of the morning they were nearing the end of their tour of the house, but had seen and heard nothing to answer any of their questions. By that time, after what seemed hours, they were doing little more than assuming a polite appearance of interest in what they were told. The most relevant part concerned the Machyn family experience during the Civil War, when the then owner had gone to fight for the king, leaving his wife to face a siege by a Roundhead army. But Katie was pretty sure that their lady was unlikely to have been around at that period. 'Thirty years too late, if the costume's right,' she murmured knowledgeably. 'And people didn't live so long in those days, on the whole.'

'Just one more room,' the housekeeper said at last, to their great relief. 'The green parlour.' Here there was more fine gilded furniture, upholstered in pale apple green to match the walls, more paintings, a fine tapestry—and above a door on the far side, a huge oil painting of a family group, father and mother and a row of children, including a babe in arms.

Josh glanced at it, came to a halt, and then

went to stand beneath it. 'That woman—the mother!' She was dressed in some sort of silvery embroidered cloth, with a lacy ruff and a small lace cap on her head; a slender graceful dark little lady, whose eyes seemed to gaze right at him with a friendly directness.

'It's the right period,' Katie said thoughtfully. She turned to Mrs Westbury. 'Have you any idea who she is?'

The housekeeper consulted her notes. 'Just a moment—ah, here we are! *A fine portrait of Sir Thomas Machyn and family, artist unknown, circa 1595. The eldest son, also Thomas (third from right, holding a hawk) inherited Haroby Court at the age of eleven on his father's death shortly after this portrait was painted.*'

'Nothing at all about the wife.' Josh sounded more frustrated than disappointed.

'And there's nothing to link her to Holywell or Durham or anything.'

'I just have this feeling.'

'Feelings aren't enough, are they?'

'No, I suppose they aren't. Though if she was widowed soon after this portrait was painted, then she'd wear black, wouldn't she? Like the lady in the garden.' He grinned suddenly. 'All right, it's fanciful stuff isn't it? What we need is a family tree or something.'

'Then we'll have to hope the county record

office has something.' Before leaving Meadhope they had phoned to book a session there for that same afternoon.

The large breakfast hadn't after all been enough to keep them going until the evening. By the end of their tour of the house, they were exhausted and hungry and by no means ready to face files of dusty papers, or whatever else the record office had in store for them; so they took themselves to a comfortable tea shop in a neighbouring village and had soup and cake and coffee, while they considered the morning's work.

'I feel really excited. I'm sure we've found her. We just need to put a name to her—'

'And a life history,' added Katie between mouthfuls of crusty bread.

'Are you OK? Are you enjoying this?'

'Oh yes—it's something really different. My life's been a bit narrow and boring the last few years or so. It feels good to be getting my teeth into something.' She took another spoonful of the leek and potato soup.

'What was he like, this Luke?'

The question startled her into silence. She laid down her spoon to give the matter some thought. 'Sweet,' she said at last. Then she hesitated again. 'It's so hard to say now. It's not that I don't remember. Just that when I look back he was so young, so uncomplicated, just a nice boy; good company, but so *young*. So was I. I've come such a long way since then and somehow I've left him behind. What would he have been like now, if it hadn't happened? I don't know—but then I'd have been different if it hadn't happened.' She looked up at him. 'Am I making any sense?'

'Yes, I think so.'

'And you—Miriam, did you say she was called? What was she like?'

Josh's face took on a dreamy reflective expression. Katie could see he was a long way from here, far from this English town, from the rain, from her.

'A little older than me, with a lot more experience of life. But so warm. Warm—yes, that was the essence of her. Lots of laughter, but always kind, loving laughter. And a deep religious faith, so she was always sure where she stood, always completely certain everything was for the best, even at the end, when…when it was hard. Children loved her. Everyone loved her. She was stubborn too, if she thought something was right—that's why she wouldn't take the AIDS drugs, the antiretroviral drugs, even when she could have done, as my wife. Unless all those who needed them could have them, then she wouldn't. So she didn't and she died. I was so angry with her. Yet she wouldn't have been Miriam if she'd done anything differently.'

'Do you believe too—do you have a religious faith? I suppose you do, having a vicar for a mother.'

'It doesn't follow, believe me! To be honest, I don't know. Sometimes I think, what good did it do for Miriam, all her faith? Other times—oh, I just don't know.'

'Do you go to church?'

'Sometimes. Quiet sort of services usually, when there's no one much there. When I can just sit at the back and no one notices.'

'Doesn't your mother mind?'

'I suppose she'd like me to believe, in the way she does. But she'd never push it, never. We always had to go to church as children—not forced exactly, it was just something we did. You accept things when you're little. But now we're adults it's up to us. What about you? Do you believe in any sort of God?'

'Not really. It was never any part of my life, religion. School assemblies—that was about the limit.'

'Boarding school?'

'Day school. Queen's College.'

'Don't know it. It was the bog-standard comp. for me. Then Leicester Uni. You? Have you been to uni?'

'I had a place at Durham. So had Luke. Different subjects, but we just had to get the grades. I guess we would have done. But—' She shrugged.

'Oh God, I'm sorry!'

'It did all seem a bit too good to be true. Anyway, I quite enjoy what I do, make up and pedicures and that sort of thing. Makes people feel good, which is nice.'

'Will you ever go to university, do you think? Fine city, Durham.'

'Oh I don't know. I have to get my head together first. I'm only just back to thinking I might take those A levels. But—well, Durham might be a step too far, too many memories and might-have-beens. Also—'

'Yes?'

'Oh, nothing! One day at a time. Who knows after that?'

'Yeah, it's the only way.' He gulped down the last of his coffee. 'Let's get back to our lady.'

At the record office, the Machyn family

papers were brought to them a few at a time and under strictly supervised conditions, because of their fragile nature. With the help of a plump kindly archivist called Sue—'I don't think anyone's ever asked to see these before!' she told them in tones of real excitement—they were able to work out which of the papers to order from the catalogue, fill in the requisite forms and wait for them to be brought to them. Then came the business of trying to decipher the strange intricate handwriting in which they were written, which was difficult even after a swift tutorial from the archivist, though once again Katie proved to have the sharper historical instinct.

It was slow laborious work, and largely fruitless, for most of the documents appeared to have nothing to do with the little family in the portrait, though the more interesting ones would often cause them to waste time following a trail that led nowhere, just out of curiosity. By the time the office was due to close, they'd found no answers to their questions about Sir Thomas Machyn's wife, but there were still many documents to work through.

'You know what this means?' Josh's rueful expression was mirrored in Katie's.

'Only too well,' she said. Another night at

the *Haroby Court Guest House*—which, unsurprisingly, was able and only too willing to accommodate them. This time they paid for rooms only. 'We have to leave early,' they gave as their excuse, so as not to hurt the feelings of their troubled host. 'We'd rather make a stop for breakfast on the way.'

Next morning, after another massive breakfast at the friendly corner café, they returned to hours of work at the record office.

And there, at long last, Katie opened the folder in front of her and gave a little squeak of excitement. 'Josh!' she hissed. 'This is a marriage contract—look: *30 April 1583, at Haroby Court, between Thomas Machyn, baronet…* No, it's a betrothal—that's an engagement, isn't it?'

Josh came to her side and together they deciphered the words. *Between Sir Thomas Machyn, baronet, and Katharine Gaunt, spinster…* Katharine! Your name!' He turned his attention back to the document. *The sum of £400, together with the manor of High Bagby in the county of Northamptonshire…* and so on and so on…Here, look: *To be settled upon her for life the manor of*—his voice suddenly grew shrill—*Holywell in the Bishopric of Durham!* He leapt up and caught Katie in his arms and they did a joyful dance about the Search Room, which brought the archivist scurrying back into the room.

Trying to talk coherently and calmly, they explained what they'd found, and she read through the document, filling out the details for them. 'This is the betrothal contract. It was as binding as a marriage. They'd have been married soon afterwards, but the settlement was the important thing in well-to-do families in those days. The jointure would be settled on her to provide for her in the event of widowhood. In this case, it would be a property already in the hands of her family. Otherwise everything she brought to the marriage would by law belong to her husband. Married women had no property rights at all during the lives of their husbands.'

'Very unfair!' exclaimed Katie.

'It doesn't look as though she was particularly wealthy. A respectable but not a brilliant match by the standards of the time. But Sir Thomas seems to have had enough for both of them. So you know something about this Holywell? Is that the house you're researching?'

'Yes. Do you think she'd have lived there before her marriage?'

She peered again at the document. 'There's nothing here to suggest she did, at least not at the time the contract was drawn up. Perhaps she was living at High Bagby. Though she may have been living away from home, wherever that was —perhaps with relations, or with people who had some family connection. Children were often sent away from home as part of their education, much as they're sent to boarding school these days, though they'd be a bit like superior servants in a great household. Why don't you look through the parish registers to see if her birth or death were registered? If not, you could try the Durham record office.'

'What about marriage records? Wouldn't that be easier?'

'You can try. But they weren't regularly kept at this period.'

They found the baptisms of her children recorded in the register of the parish church at Haroby, and that of her husband early in 1540, but not hers. 'So he was 43 when he married. Not young by the standards of the time. Maybe he'd been married before.' Sue carefully turned the pages of the volume before them. 'Yes— here we have the baptisms of two children— and their burial. Oh, and his wife, Anne, died in childbirth in 1560. A long gap before he married again—surprising. Let's see...Oh no, here's another child, born 1579, a daughter. And another death in childbirth, Mary: a second wife then. So Katharine was his *third* wife! Perhaps it was a love-match, which would explain the small dowry. Or he was desperate for a male heir.'

'And what about the Gunpowder plot? How can we find out if any of them were involved?'

'Try the *Calendar of State Papers Domestic*, which you can access on line. That would be your best bet. Then there are recusant records, fines for non-attendance at church, that kind of thing.'

'But the children were christened in church!'

'Many Catholics hedged their bets, to avoid fines. Sometimes friendly Anglican clergy would enter them in the church register even if they hadn't actually used the church. Or they'd be bribed to do so.'

Their searches revealed the baptisms of the children in the portrait, born in swift succession following the marriage: Thomas, the heir, in 1584, and then eight more, some of whom died in infancy. 'Poor woman!' sighed Katie. 'She was pretty well non-stop pregnant for—what? Ten whole years.' She grinned. 'Maybe she murdered her husband to get a breathing space!'

'And now she can't rest, but paces the floor of Holywell in an agony of guilt!'

'Except that none of this seems to have happened at Holywell.'

'Perhaps she died there.' They had already found Sir Thomas's death, recorded at St Mary's church, Haroby, in the early spring of 1595—of an apoplexy, it was noted. But though they searched through decades of records, they found none of their lady's death.

'We'll just have to go back to Durham and look there,' said Josh. He felt a twinge of regret at the thought that this interlude would soon be over. 'You know, I might even miss our guest house. Good for a laugh if nothing else.'

'I guess if we'd stayed any longer the atmosphere would have got to us. You can only find so much to laugh at in a place like that.'

'Nurse Hutchinson's just rung,' Alastair said as Rosalind stepped through the door after a long and difficult PCC meeting. She saw that he had his coat on, as if about to go out. 'Mother's had another fall.'

Rosalind put down her bag but left her own coat on. 'Is it serious?'

'She's not in hospital. I think it was more a matter of not being able to get up once she was down. Miss Hutchinson got her to a chair and made her a cup of tea and then phoned me.

She'd called round with a book she'd offered to lend her and found her there. Goodness knows how long she'd been like that.'

They drove quickly round to Valley Close, where Phyllis Hutchinson opened Jessie's door to them. 'She's a bit shaken, as you'd expect, but I think that's the worst of it.'

Alastair went through to the lounge, where his mother, looking pale and exhausted, sat in her favourite chair with the air of someone who had no intention of moving from it ever again. 'Now then, Mother, what have you been up to?'

She frowned at the jocular tone. 'Don't patronise me, Alastair. I had a wee fall, that's all. It is fortunate that Miss Hutchinson chanced to call round. I should not have to depend on my good neighbour. If you did not grudge me the little time it would take to look in each day after work, then this need not have happened. Nor should I have been without help for so long.'

The fall certainly hasn't softened her, Rosalind thought—which was something of a relief. On the one occasion when Jessie had suffered a really serious fall, breaking her hip as a result, she had, temporarily, become almost submissive.

'I've been telling Jessie she should make use of the council's very excellent alarm service,' Phyllis Hutchinson broke in. 'I fully intend to do so if ever I become a little unsure on my feet.'

This was the very suggestion that Rosalind and Alastair had often made to Jessie, with no success at all. Would her neighbour be better received?

'I am not unsure on my feet. I tripped, that's all.'

'Of course—it can happen to any of us! But an alarm on a cord around your neck would be an added reassurance. There's someone always on call, even if you can't reach the telephone. Trained people, two of them at a time, who can help you to your feet and provide whatever is necessary.'

'It is a family responsibility, not a matter for the social services,' retorted Jessie; and then, perhaps realising how ungracious that must sound, added, 'Of course, I am very grateful for your help. It was fortunate that you called when you did. However, it should not have fallen to you to help me. It is not your responsibility.'

Phyllis raised her eyebrows at Rosalind. 'I suggest you give it some thought all the same.' Then, before Jessie could say anything more on the matter, she changed the subject, 'Now, are you sure you wouldn't like me to call the doctor? Just to check you over.'

'I doubt if anyone would come out at this

time of night,' Rosalind murmured to Alastair. 'I think it would be an ambulance or nothing. Or do we take her to the out-of-hours service?'

'Maybe we should call an ambul—'

'Don't mutter—I can't hear what you say! Of course I don't need a doctor!' She pressed her hands down on the arms of the chair and tried to rise, sinking back almost at once. 'Now, I should like to go to bed.'

They thanked Jessie's neighbour warmly for her help. Once she'd returned home, they set to work to get the old woman upstairs and to bed, which took a very long time and left all three of them exhausted. 'I'll stay here tonight, just in case,' Alastair said to Rosalind as they stood on the landing afterwards, 'if you don't mind waiting here while I just go and get some things.'

'We've got to persuade her to have a stair lift. With that and the alarm, she'd get her independence back. Though I'm not convinced that's what she wants.'

'No, what she really wants is the two of us at her beck and call.' They began to descend the stairs. 'I'm beginning to think that we're just going to have to overrule her and get a stair lift put in whether she likes it or not.'

'Can we do that? Legally, I mean? We

certainly won't get her to wear an alarm round her neck if she doesn't want to. I'm afraid we're going to have to keep trying to persuade her.'

The following morning, Jessie seemed very much herself again, but was sufficiently shaken and bruised to agree that Rosalind should take her to the doctor; who insisted on referring her to a geriatric specialist. Being of a generation who regarded doctors with respect, she allowed the arrangements to be made, though once back in the waiting room out of earshot of her GP, she expressed outrage. 'Does he think I'm senile?' she demanded as Rosalind helped her back into the car.

'Of course not! I suppose anyone over sixty counts as geriatric—I'm nearly there myself. And you'll be ninety soon, remember. I guess this specialist will look at the whole person, not just one bit of you, which can only be a good thing, can't it? You want to make sure you're fit for your big party next year.'

'You know I don't want a fuss. There's no great merit in growing old.'

And wouldn't we all know about it if we neglected to make a fuss, Rosalind acknowledged wryly, but all she said was, 'If this appointment makes sure you're as well as you can be, that can't be bad can it?'

'Hmph!'

'I guess there are going to be endless tests as a result of all this,' Rosalind reported to Alastair that evening.

'If need be I'll take some time off so as to do my share of hospital ferrying. Did you try mentioning the stair lift, alarm and all that again?'

'I did, and so did Doctor Stephenson. She didn't actually say no to him, but you know that expression of hers?'

'Only too well. Och well! Let's hope that appointment comes through quickly. If there is something wrong with her, more than just lack of balance—and I think you're probably right about that—then the sooner it's identified the better.'

Chapter Twelve

'Katie! You're back!'

She bounced into the kitchen, lighting it with her glowing face, her smile, with a sense of vibrant life and energy—not unlike Tiger, Juliet thought, watching how the kitten danced around her in greeting. Katie kissed Juliet and then perched on the edge of the table. 'Oh, it's been great—you can't imagine! Just wait till you hear what we've found! We've had such a laugh too. It's been so good to be able to laugh again.'

Juliet felt as if a cruel hand had clutched her heart. When had Katie ever looked like this before—? Long ago, when she and Luke had first been together, in the untainted joy of first love…Could she be falling in love again, with this boy who looked nothing like Luke, who had no connection with her beyond a chance acquaintanceship? *No! Don't let it happen*!

She sat in silence while Katie chattered on about the places they'd visited, the people they'd spoken to, the things they'd discovered. Eventually, her unresponsiveness must have cut through Katie's exuberance, for the girl suddenly fell silent, studying Juliet's face. 'Is something wrong? Has something else happened while we've been away?'

'Something else? What do you mean?'

A guilty shadow crossed Katie's face. 'I overheard Leo saying something to you the other day. It made me think there was a bit more to all this than you were letting on, so I badgered Josh into telling me what he'd heard —'

But it was not Josh's indiscretion that troubled Juliet; it was the words Katie had used. *We've* been away, she'd said; not *I've*—the distinction struck her to the heart. 'I see,' she said stiffly. 'But no, nothing else has happened. Everything's fine.' She stood up. 'Let's have supper.'

'I'll give you a hand.'

'No thanks. It's all ready. You go and get yourself settled in.' Her tone was so dismissive that Katie was hurt and disturbed. Something was clearly wrong, but nothing that she could put her finger on, nothing tangible.

'Don't you want to hear what we found?'

'You can tell me while we eat.'

Leo joined them for the meal, during which he talked endlessly about his work on the door, and his plans and hopes for it, while Juliet sat tight-lipped and strained and Katie struggled to make polite responses, all the time wishing he would go so that she could try and prise from

Juliet the reason for her sudden change of manner. There was no opportunity even to tell her about the results of the most recent research.

After the meal, Leo took what remained of his glass of wine up to his room—'Want to check online for anywhere that might have the right door'—and Katie rushed to help Juliet load the dishwasher.

Juliet shouldered her out of the way. 'I can manage. You go and sit down with a book or something.'

Katie recoiled at the dismissive tone. 'I haven't told you what we found out yet—'

'Go on then.'

It was hardly encouraging, but Katie told Juliet about their findings in Warwickshire, though stiffly, sketchily, with none of the eager enthusiasm she'd shown when she'd first returned to Holywell. Juliet's response was equally stiff, though now and then her expression revealed a trace of excitement or surprise—in particular when Katie told her how they'd found the portrait and then the name of the lady in it. 'Josh was so sure she was the one —and then to find her name in the record and then the link to Holywell on top of that. You can imagine—!'

This time, Juliet actually smiled. 'I can.'

'We did a little dance round the record office. Not quite the thing in those stuffy surroundings, but still. We were so excited!'

The chill enveloped them again. 'I imagine you were.' Then, after a little pause during which Juliet bent to arrange two saucepans in the lower basket of the dishwasher: 'Luke would so have enjoyed doing all this with you.'

Would he? Katie wondered. He'd never had much interest in history. But then by now he would have changed in so many ways, simply because experience, life, would have left its mark on him. Who knew what he would have thought of it all? 'I suppose he would,' she heard herself say. Then she found herself questioning whether any of this would have happened had he lived. Would Juliet have heard those strange sounds, would they have troubled her as they did? More to the point, would she and Leo ever have come here at all, hundreds of miles removed from the old familiar world that had been wrenched from them when Luke died? Perhaps they would, once Luke had left home and established an independent life for himself. They might still have wanted a project for their later years, for their retirement. It was obvious that Leo had been dissatisfied with the constrictions of his working life, and he had certainly always enjoyed working with his hands, even when Luke was alive and he'd had so little time. Katie recalled how he'd once made a bedside cabinet for his son's bedroom, which even to her inexperienced eyes had been the work of a true craftsman. But somehow she doubted if it would ever have been quite like this, without that dreadful accident.

Then, abruptly, she guessed why Juliet had suddenly become so withdrawn, even cold; why she'd made the reference to Luke that had been almost accusatory in its tone: she was jealous for Luke's sake of her friendship with Josh, disapproving that she should have even a mere friend who was not Luke. Katie knew she had to put things right, as quickly as she could. She searched her memory for something to call on. 'Do you remember that ball we went to? When Luke dressed as a Cavalier? I went as Nell Gwynne, didn't I?'

Juliet's face lit up, soft and tender. 'Oh yes— the charity ball, for the ovarian cancer charity. We couldn't go, could we? Leo had some conference to attend. You looked wonderful, the two of you together. Luke had only known you a few weeks.' She fell silent, her thoughts clearly running back to that now-so-distant past. Then she laughed. 'He had a wig, didn't he? Shoulder length, all black curls? It really rather suited him! Oh, wouldn't he have been at home here!'

'He would have been in his element,' said Kate, while she thought: *No, he wouldn't—he'd have hated this place, so far from all the excitement of city life, from his friends, from everything.* Somehow the thought of him seemed so irrelevant here, having nothing to do with Holywell and all it meant to Juliet and Leo. Hastily she resumed her reminiscence. 'It was very uncomfortable, that wig—much too hot. He took it off after about half an hour, said he'd turned into a Roundhead instead! I teased him and said Nell Gwynne would never stomach a Roundhead and I'd find myself someone else. So he said he was a converted Roundhead, who'd lost his principles with his heart.' They had indeed been been happy then, light-hearted, carefree. They'd been good times, so very long ago now. But though she could recall them, remember the laughter, she could not recapture them in all their sunny insouciance. Those days were over, for ever. She was a different person, as was Juliet. They could not bring back the past, nor relive it. Nor, now, did she want to.

'We're going to Durham again tomorrow, Josh and I. Now we know the lady's name, we hope we can find her in the records up here. Maybe we'll find out if she actually lived here at all.'

'She did. I'm sure of it.'

'So's Josh. But it would be good to have it confirmed.'

'Yes.' Juliet gazed at Katie for a few moments, then said, 'You wouldn't like to help me with stripping the plaster tomorrow—?' She must have read Katie's expression (though the girl tried to mask it), for she added quickly, 'No, of course not. You go and do your research. You'll enjoy it.'

Katie wondered whether to put aside her own feelings and agree to stay for Juliet's sake, then decided against it. There were limits to what she would do to soothe Luke's grieving mother.

'Thanks! I will!'

Chapter Thirteen

Juliet spent two hours in the garden, seizing the moment while Leo was out. Last night had been another bad one, so she needed the healing that gardening brought her. It was strange, she reflected; darkness brought terror so great that she would wake feeling she must somehow escape from here, would wonder what vindictive fate had made them buy this place, what could have possessed them to move here. Yet in daylight—except when in the hall—she felt only a sense of peace and hope, a feeling that here she was truly at home, as far as ever she could be in a world without Luke. Above all, the garden was the place where she felt most hopeful that one day life would be worth living again. But was it going to be possible to continue to live here so long as the nights brought such increasing horrors? What if they should begin to seep into her days, spread out from the hall and the ancient doorway to the rest of the house? *'Sounds can't hurt you,'* Leo had said, and common sense told her that was true, but it didn't *feel* true.

She kept an eye on the time, so as to be changed, the tools put away, before Leo returned. Besides, it had begun to spot with rain. Indoors, changed, she made herself coffee and picked up a pile of post from the doorstep, sorry that she'd missed the postman. He would have driven up in his red van—just like Postman Pat, so Katie had said the first time she saw him, and equally friendly, always ready to talk. Today there was a letter for her, a personal, handwritten letter, with a blurred postmark. She opened it, wondering; and saw that the card inside, with its tasteful flower picture and neatly written message, was from Celia Warriner— Celia, once one of her dearest friends, who had let her down when she most needed her. She was tempted to tear it up unread, but in the end began to skim through it. She would throw it away afterwards.

I've only just heard that you've moved away. I missed my chance to say how sorry I am. I think I said all the wrong things when you most needed me. It's very hard to know what's the right thing to say, and you know how clumsily impulsive I am—I'm always putting my foot in it. If anything I said hurt you or caused you any kind of pain, please believe me I never meant that to happen and I am most deeply sorry.

If you can forgive, email—or better still give me a call some time. Love you lots, C xxxx

She found the tears spring to her eyes. How stupid! Celia had hurt her deeply. Why should she be so moved by this attempt at reconciliation, which she had neither wanted nor asked for?

She took the letter into the garden and sat on the old wooden bench under the kitchen window, holding it in her hands, going over the past. In her pain and anger she had thought Celia's behaviour unforgivable. But if she'd been in Celia's place, would she have done any better, in the days before she knew what it was to lose a child? And was clumsiness really the worst failure of friendship?

Uneasily, she recalled that Celia was not the only one who had offended against the laws of friendship; what of her own behaviour towards Rosalind all those years ago? Or were there in fact no laws, was the essential thing about friendship that you could forgive because you knew that person so well, loved them so well, that you understood there was no malice behind the words, only a momentary lapse?

She cast a hard look back through the years at the teenage Juliet, guilty of something far worse than a momentary lapse without malicious intent. Her own offence had not been one of clumsy words, but of mean thoughts, snobbishness, a deliberate tactic to exclude her oldest, most faithful friend from her life. Wasn't that far worse than Celia's impulsiveness?

Yet it seemed as if Rosalind had been able to forgive her, and even offer a renewed friendship —But then forgiveness was in her job description. So was the readiness to listen, to care, to offer friendship to all who came her way and were in need; as Juliet had been in need. Even that day in Durham could be interpreted simply as an example of a good vicar, caring for a troubled parishioner. It was helpful, it had meant a great deal at the time, but that did not make it true friendship, of the kind that had once bound them so closely together. Could she ever hope to retrieve that friendship?

On impulse, she jumped in the car and drove to Meadhope, and then thought how foolish she'd feel if Rosalind happened to be out.

She was in. 'Juliet! What a lovely surprise. I've just made some coffee. Will you join me?'

'I've just had some, thanks.' The reply sounded churlish, but if Rosalind minded she didn't show it.

'Let's go into my study then.' She ushered her into a room that was both tranquil and purposeful. Books lined the walls, works on theology or forms of worship, hymn books and prayer books, all the tools of Rosalind's trade. There was a laptop on the desk, with a suitably meditative screen-saver, a little table on which lay a copy of the *Church Times* and Meadhope's parish magazine; and a comfortable armchair in which Juliet took her seat. In spite of the warmth of the welcome—perhaps because of it—she was beginning to wish she hadn't come; to wonder indeed what idiocy had brought her here. She stared down at her hands, conscious that Rosalind had taken a seat facing her and was waiting quietly for her to speak.

'There's something I need to know, but it's not easy…I think I know the answer, to be honest. It's clear enough—' A pause, then she burst out: 'I'm just a parishioner to you aren't I?' She wished at once that it hadn't sounded so accusing. 'You can't help it, looking at me that way. It's what you do, what you have to do. What I'm saying is—to you, I'm not really a friend, just a parishioner in need of support.'

There was a little pause, which seemed only to confirm what she had said. Then Rosalind answered slowly and thoughtfully, as if, rather than evading the issue, she was giving it the most careful consideration so that she could come up with a scrupulously truthful answer.

'At first, when we met, it was mixed; and yes, I did come to see you the first time partly as a parish priest calling on a new parishioner. But very soon—No, I think it was always there. I'd forgotten how close we were at school—and how much I missed you when you left.' Rosalind reached for her mug from the desk, though she made no move to drink from it. 'It's hard to have real friendships, as a parish priest. You mustn't show favouritism to anyone, and of course that's what friendship is, favouring someone over another, because something clicks between you. But with you living a bit out of the village it's easier. Especially as you're not in my congregation either.'

Juliet ventured a smile. 'Oh, so the last thing you want is to get me into church?'

Rosalind laughed. 'Probably depends which hat I'm wearing.' Then: 'We were so close once. I know we were only children, but it felt like a friendship that would last for ever. I think I would have liked it to have done. I don't quite remember what happened. But it's wonderful to be given a second chance.'

'For me too...' A long pause, then: 'Because it wasn't just chance that it didn't last.' She saw Rosalind's questioning look and forced herself to the admission that might even now end this renewed friendship once and for all. 'I meant it to, at first. Then I had new friends. You know how it is, you want to fit in, impress them. And anyone who doesn't fit—'

'And I didn't fit?'

She nodded. Would Rosalind fill in the rest, understand—even forgive?

There was a long silence, during which she could see Rosalind taking in what she said, hearing what she had left unsaid. 'And that's why you stopped writing—and why I thought you'd left the area. I know—or I do now. I really hadn't remembered any of it, but my mother had, when I mentioned it to her. I suppose mothers feel their children's hurts even more than the children do. Anyway, it clearly didn't leave any scars on my psyche. As you said once, girls can be very cruel. And having seen it with my own children, I know how hard peer pressure is to resist. We all want to belong. But it was a long time ago, and we *have* been given a second chance. I feel now as if there's never been a break.'

Juliet found her eyes filling with tears, though she tried to smile. 'Thank you for that.'

Rosalind touched her arm. 'Do you really think I'd harbour a grudge over something you did when we were little more than children— even if I had remembered it? We've both come a very long way since then. I suppose we're the same people, but we're very different too. The thing that does remain is whatever it was in each of us that felt a kinship with the other. The thing that made us friends.'

Then she reached out her arms, drawing Juliet to her in the warmest of hugs; bringing to a close all that remained of the long-past rift.

'Talking of friends—' Juliet said at last, and told Rosalind about Celia's letter.

'So you'll get in touch with her again?'

'Yes. I was unreasonable.'

'The bereaved often are.'

'Even so. I have a feeling I'd have been as hopelessly tactless as she was if our roles had been reversed. When you haven't lived through it—' Her eyes fell on the family photo on Rosalind's desk: Alastair with their two children, a close and loving trio. 'Rosie, can I ask you something? Has Josh said anything about Katie?'

'What sort of a thing?'

'What he thinks of her.'

Rosalind scrutinised her. 'You mean—is there anything between them, apart from a shared interest in your ghostly lady? I really don't know. They seem to enjoy each other's company, but Josh is still very raw after losing Miriam.'

'I thought Katie was too. She told me once

she'd never love anyone as she'd loved Luke.'

'I imagine that's true, in its way. He was her first love, wasn't he? That's bound to be special. But realistically it might not have lasted. They were very young.' She could see the hurt in Juliet's eyes. 'I'm sorry, that's not what you wanted to hear. I may be entirely wrong. But losing the love of your life at eighteen isn't like losing your child. Nothing like it.'

'No—no, I suppose it isn't. I wanted it to be —'

'I know. I think I understand. But even if it's true, it doesn't in any way mean she feels anything much for Josh. I imagine they're just enjoying a bit of uncomplicated fun.'

Juliet left soon afterwards, feeling greatly comforted, with Rosalind's parting words in her ear: 'If things get difficult, as they will; remember—any time you need me, day or night, I'm always there for you. It's what friends are for—' She smiled. 'And, yes, priests as well.'

Rosalind's heart sank as she steered Jessie with a gentle hand into the allotted hospital waiting area. There were only two seats free, and those not together. It was going to take a very long time. She pushed from her mind all thoughts of wasted time, of the things she could be doing this afternoon, and concentrated on Jessie. After all, that was why she was here, since Alastair had an important meeting and couldn't take the time off himself.

'You sit here, Jessie—I'll take that seat.' Jessie sat down, while Rosalind moved towards the only other empty place, further along the row.

'Here, I'll move up and you can sit together.'

Rosalind realised she knew the woman who had intervened: Michelle Brooks, one of the teachers at Meadhope's primary school. She took the vacated seat. 'What brings you here?'

'Mam.' Michelle gestured towards the elderly woman at her side, who was gazing vacantly across the passage at the various notices about the right way to wash hands, help for dementia patents, keeping appointments and not behaving aggressively towards nursing staff. She showed no sign that she was taking any of their messages in. 'You too?' Rosalind nodded. 'They're doing some tests. More tests.'

'Looks as though we'll have a long wait.'

'It's always slow, this clinic.' Michelle nodded towards the board where the estimated delays in appointment times were written up. 'Two hours. Which likely means more. They don't put anything up until they're over the half hour. Our appointment was half past, so we've an hour and twenty minutes to go.' She sighed. 'I should be teaching my ten-year-olds about the second world war this afternoon. But there we are.'

'I sometimes get the impression that's the only history they ever do these days. That and Henry the Eighth.'

'We did him last year. But I know what you mean. I'm trying to get a different angle. I'm thinking of getting some older people in to talk about their wartime experiences. There must be lots of pensioners in Meadhope and around who have memories of the war, in their different ways. I don't mean just those who served in the forces. What it was like to experience an air raid, dealing with evacuees, how women's lives were changed by it all. That sort of thing.'

'Oh, Jessie could tell you some stories!' Rosalind glanced at her mother-in-law. 'You had quite an adventurous war, didn't you?'

'I did my duty,' said Jessie stiffly.

Michelle leaned over. 'How would you like to come into school and tell us a bit about it?'

Jessie looked startled. 'I don't know…I lived in Scotland then.'

'That doesn't matter. Sometimes we're given the impression the war only affected London— the blitz and all that. It's good if they get a wider picture.'

'We had our air raids. I remember the raid on the Forth bridge in 1939. I joined up soon afterwards. The Wrens, the Women's—'

'Oh that sounds just the sort of thing that would really interest them! Do think about coming in to tell us about it! The kids would love to hear your stories. You'd have to be ready for lots of questions, mind.'

Rosalind saw the spark of curiosity in Jessie's face, warring with her usual assumption that nothing of interest ever happened to her. It would have seemed just what she needed— except that in her uncertain state of health she might find it hard to cope with anything so strenuous.

Then Michelle's mother was called—'By, that was quick! They must have caught up'— and the conversation ceased.

'They say she's suffering from—now, what are they called?—transient ischaemic attacks,' Rosalind told Alastair that evening, as they lay side by side in bed. They had each had meetings that evening, so—as happened too often—this was the first time they had been together since breakfast. 'They're a kind of mini-stroke, short-lived, but liable to cause falls, confusion and such like.'

'And can they lead to proper strokes?'

'I think it means she's at greater risk, yes. She's been put on medication for it, but realistically she's going to need keeping an eye on.'

'Then she needs some sort of additional care, as a matter of urgency. An alarm at the very least.'

'And one of us looking in every day, as far as possible.'

'I'm afraid so. But that alarm is really urgent.'

'Then which of us is going to tackle her about it this time?'

'Josh?' He saw the startled look on Rosalind's face. 'Why not? She's fond of him. She's certainly closer to him than to either of us —or at least, she has an easier relationship with him.'

'Except where her attitude to Miriam's concerned.'

'Surprisingly, I think he doesn't hold that against her. He puts it down to her age and background.'

'That's true, up to a point, though it doesn't mean he hasn't been hurt by it. Anyway, it's worth a try. When he comes up for air again from all his research, we'll see if he's willing to tackle his Gran.'

As they turned to go to sleep, Alastair suddenly said, 'This research of Josh's—he's getting very enthusiastic. Do you think part of the attraction is his companion?'

'Katie? Funny you should ask that. I had Juliet here this morning, worried about exactly that, that Katie might be losing her heart to Josh. I told her I guessed they were just enjoying a bit of normal young company. Which is all I think it is, for the time being anyway.'

'All the same, it would be good if he could find someone else.'

'But two damaged people together? I'm not sure about that. I know it probably means they have a lot in common, but—Oh, it's much too soon to start speculating, or worrying.'

'And you know that whatever happens we'll make the best of it.' He turned to face her, putting his arms about her. 'There's a lot to be said for enjoying life while you can, isn't there?'

'Now what can you possibly mean by that I wonder?' Rosalind asked, as she snuggled closer.

Josh, his eyes on the microfilm reader, gave a squeak of excitement: 'At last! Here it is! Baptism, at St Luke's church Meadhope, on 30

April 1569, of Katharine Gaunt of Holywell. She must have been much younger than Sir Thomas! No wonder we couldn't find her baptism yesterday. We were looking much too early. When was she married? 1583?'

Katie glanced at the notes they'd made in Warwickshire. 'That's right. So she must have been—what? Just fourteen, to his forty three! Goodness! I wonder if she loved him? Could it have been a love match with that age difference?'

'Who knows? I don't suppose love mattered in those days. Or maybe *he* loved her anyway.'

'Dirty old man!' Shuddering, Katie moved her chair closer to Josh the better to see his screen. 'Here, there's another Gaunt— Katharine again! Is she the same one? Died in childbirth, May 1572—oh, it can't be our Katharine, this one was twenty four. And a day later, Nicholas, baptised 1576. Son of that Katharine—our Katharine's younger brother, do you think?' She scribbled down the details while Josh continued to scour the register. 'So, it looks as though our Katherine's mother died when she was only three. Poor little thing. Any more Gaunts? Any Machyns?'

'No Machyns so far. Another Gaunt here though, a death: Henry Gaunt, gentleman, died of a fever aged 54, February 1577. Do you suppose that was their father?'

'Could have been.' She sketched a speculative family tree. 'That all fits together nicely. Hey, maybe that's when they moved to the Midlands, when their father died! No parents left, so someone had to look after them. But that would make their connection with Holywell very limited. They could hardly have remembered it afterwards.'

'Perhaps the brother came back here to live. Or Katharine after her husband's death—it was her jointure wasn't it?'

'But if her eldest son was still at Haroby wouldn't she have stayed there with him? He'd inherited it after all. And he was only eleven. He'd need his Mum.'

'There's no hint either way so far. We can only guess.'

They found no more that day, so gathered up their notes and emerged from the subterranean office into the clear light of the November afternoon. 'If she was born at Holywell and grew up there, do you suppose she spent the rest of her life wishing to be back there? Do you suppose that's what the sobbing's all about?'

'Hmm. Could be. But if they did move away

after their father's death, I should think they'd hardly have remembered it.' He grinned suddenly. 'Listen to us, talking about it as if it was all a normal everyday thing!'

'Fun though,' Katie said. 'But what now?'

'Calendar of State Papers, like the lady said. Come back to mine and we'll get on line. See if there's anything in the Gunpowder plot story.'

Back at the rectory, Josh brought his laptop down to the dining room and they sat at the table, with a growing cluster of tea and coffee mugs beside them. Finding the right website was astonishingly easy, and they quickly moved to the list of documents for November 1605, finding instructions for the torture of Guy Fawkes, accounts of the pursuit of the other plotters, countless reports of witnesses and suspects examined, all flowing back to the Earl of Salisbury, secretary of state to King James.

'Look! Here, on November 8th: *John Mycock to Salisbury: Nicholas Gaunt, servant to Robert Catesby, reported to be riding north. Seen near Ripon.*'

Katie's smile was enchanted. 'Her brother! It has to be!'

'Hang on—look at this: *William James, Dean of Durham: examination of Toby Machyn, formerly servant to Robert Catesby, concerning the whereabouts of Nicholas Gaunt.* Didn't you say Catesby was the leader of the plotters?'

'And Toby Machyn—wasn't that one of Katharine's sons? Yes, he's here, in my notes. But 'servant'? Can that be right? Both him and his uncle?'

'Remember what Sue said, at Warwick—He could just have been living in the household as part of his education, maybe because his uncle was there too. How old would he be?'

'Let's see—Toby, baptised at Haroby 1589. He'd have been sixteen. But he was examined in Durham. Doesn't that show he was living there at the time?'

They gazed at each other, eyes shining. 'It has to be, doesn't it? It all makes sense!'

Katie giggled. 'Or not, if you look at it another way!'

Later, when Katie had returned to Holywell to Juliet's less than warm reception, Josh put his head round the door of his mother's study. 'Can you be interrupted, Mum?'

'Of course.'

He sat down on the comfortable armchair she had ready for troubled parishioners. 'This ghost thing—I've been trying to make sense of it.'

Rosalind continued to listen, her expression

encouraging, though she knew better than to say anything.

It was a moment or two before Josh went on, hesitantly, not looking at his mother, 'When Miriam died, I looked at her lying there, when they'd laid her out. She'd looked so peaceful at the moment of death. But then, all tidied up, it was as if she wasn't like herself any more. She wasn't there—not the person I loved. She'd become a husk, an empty husk. I remember thinking it was all right with her, that she'd gone somewhere wonderful, that she was at peace and happy, as she really believed she would be. I believed it with my whole heart then. But now —it's hard to remember what that felt like, let alone believe it. And if it's true that spirits can stay and haunt a place—what if she isn't at rest at all, not even in the most basic sense of lying quiet in the grave?'

'Has anything happened to make you think that might be the case?'

'No—no, not at all. Sometimes I wish it would. To be haunted by her, to have her with me again—' His voice roughened to silence and he swallowed hard.

'I think you can be sure that all is well with her, just as you felt at first.' His mother's voice was infinitely gentle.

'Do you ever doubt there's a life after death?'

'Long ago, maybe, when I was questioning everything. But not for very many years, no.'

'But if there are ghosts, what then? It means that all the teaching about heaven and hell or whatever isn't right, that it's left something out.'

'All religious teaching leaves something out, at best. There's so much we don't know. It may even be that one day science will fill in the gaps and find an explanation for many strange phenomena. Who knows? But whatever you and Juliet have seen or heard at Holywell, I don't think that has any bearing on Miriam and where she is now.' She reached out and took his hands in hers. 'From all you've said I couldn't be more sure of anything. All's well with Miriam.' She saw that he had accepted the reassurance, like a small boy waking from a nightmare to his mother's loving, soothing words. 'As for what's been happening at Holywell, I don't know what it is, but I doubt if it has anything to do with unquiet souls seeking peace.'

At this point Alastair followed a tap on the door by putting his head round it. 'Ah, there you are, Josh. Has your Mum been filling you in about your Gran?'

'No—no, what about her? Is she all right? She hasn't had another fall?'

'No, not at all, but—'

'Because that's another thing—I've been wondering if I should try getting her to think about an alarm. It would be such a relief to know she had someone to call on if she had another fall.'

His parents looked at one another. 'Funny you should say that—' said Alastair.

Chapter Fourteen

'Hi Gran!'

Jessie peered round the wing of her chair. 'Joshua! What a pleasure!' Then she saw he wasn't alone.

'This is Katie. We've been doing some research together. I thought you'd like to meet her. She's from London.'

Katie held out her hand, greeting her with an impeccable politeness that clearly delighted the old woman.

'We shall have a cup of tea.' Jessie got to her feet. 'Then you can tell me all about this research of yours.'

The hour passed agreeably for Jessie as she listened to their thoroughly expurgated account —no mention of ghosts, of sounds in the night, of a lady encountered in a dream. Their tale was all of simple historical research, entered into out of curiosity and for amusement, and their industry and thoroughness clearly impressed Jessie. At the end, Katie loaded the tray with the tea things. 'I'll take these through and wash them up. You can have a little quality time with your grandson.' Josh got up to close the door behind her.

'What a charming girl!' Jessie gave a

knowing smile. 'I can see where this is going!'

'Can you? I can't. We're friends, with a mutual interest, that's all.'

'It's important to have matters in common. Those mixed marriages are always a mistake. It wouldn't have lasted, you know.'

Fond though he was of his grandmother, and in spite of the consoling tone of her voice, the callousness of the remark took Josh's breath away, so that for several moments he was quite unable to say anything at all, still less the things he'd planned to say. She'd hinted at these views before, but never quite so bluntly. Then, forcing himself to make allowances for her age and the narrowness of her upbringing, he bit back the sharp retort that sprang to his lips and said very carefully, trying to sound casual, 'Don't get your hopes up, Gran. I'm not ready to face a serious relationship again yet awhile.'

He sat down on the stool that stood close to her chair. 'Gran, there's something I've been wanting to say to you.' He took her thin, veined hand in his. 'I'm really worried about you, you know.' He saw her cast a questioning look in his direction. 'You've always been such a strong independent lady. It's something I really admire in you.'

'I have no intention of relinquishing my

independence, you can be sure of that!'

'I should hope not! I'd hate that.'

'Then what are you worried about?'

'Let me tell you a story, Gran. There's an old lady I knew when I was at uni. She—'

'University, Joshua! I do so dislike these sloppy modern ways of speaking!'

'Sorry Gran. Anyway, this old lady, she was was my landlady at the time. She reminded me of you in lots of ways, though she was a lot younger, only in her seventies. She had a daughter lived nearby, who kept an eye on her, but of course being an independent sort of person, she didn't want to be fussed over. Anyway, this daughter went on holiday with her family. And while she was away, unknown to her, something terrible happened to her mother. It wasn't until she got home again that she called round and found her dead on the floor. They thought she'd had a fall and couldn't get up and then just died. It must have been truly horrible for all of them., knowing she died like that, all alone, with no one to help. It doesn't bear thinking of.'

He saw the shadow pass over her face. 'That's not going to happen to me!'

'But it could, if things went badly wrong. There can't always be someone around to help, especially if you can't let them know you're in trouble. Sometimes people have strokes or heart attacks when it's really important to get medical help quickly, especially if they're going to be able to make a complete recovery. If you had one of those alarms we wouldn't have to worry about you.'

'Has your mother put you up to this?'

'No she hasn't. Though I know she's worried too—'

'In case she might have to face up to her responsibilities!'

'No, for your sake, truly, believe me. And of course Dad's very worried too. And so am I. We don't want you to end up as a permanent invalid who has to go into a home because she needs full-time care.'

'I have no intention of going into a home so long as I have family to care for me!'

'But Mum and Dad haven't got nursing experience. It's very hard lifting people who've fallen, very heavy work. That's why these alarms are good. They have two trained people to do the lifting and all the proper emergency equipment. It would be much more comfortable for you too. Being hauled around by someone who's not really strong enough can't be much fun. It could even make things worse.'

Jessie's silence convinced him that his words were making an impression on her.

'Will you think about it, Gran? And about a stair lift too perhaps, for those days when you feel a bit too tired to manage the stairs?'

'I make no promises—'

'Of course not. I'm not asking you to. Just to think about it, maybe make some enquiries.'

'I do not wish to be beholden to strangers.'

'You won't be. You've paid your taxes all your life; it's time you had something back. It's your right. In any case, I guess you have to pay something for the alarm system, and certainly for the stair lift. Anyway, if you want any help with anything, just let me know.'

'I will.' She patted Josh's hand. 'You're a good lad. I think it might be a good idea if you were to make enquiries for me, from whoever deals with these things. So as not to trouble your parents.' So as not to have to admit that they were right; or to appear to capitulate…

Josh gave a conspiratorial wink. 'Enough said, Gran. It'll be between you and me. But I'll get it sorted.' He stood up. 'I'd better go or they'll wonder where I am.'

Jessie held up her cheek for his kiss, adding, 'We understand each other then. Now, I hope you're going to bring that bonny girl to see me again soon!'

Later, as they walked back towards the rectory, Josh told Katie what his grandmother had said about her, which made her laugh. 'She's got us married off already, I bet.' She saw the alarm in her companion's face. 'Don't worry, I certainly haven't. I have so enjoyed all this research, and you're great to be with—'

'But? Like me, it's too soon for anyone else?'

'I don't think it's that exactly. It's more that —well, I want to move on, put what's past behind me. It's very hard when I know Juliet in particular values me keeping in touch. I nearly didn't come up this time, for all they'd been begging me to, even before they moved. I was beginning to feel I was getting my life together. Don't get me wrong, I really loved Luke. I shan't ever forget him. But it was a long time ago, and I've changed such a lot, partly because of what happened. I'm very fond of Leo and Juliet, but I can't live in the past for ever.'

'Does that mean you'll be going back to London soon?' He was surprised to feel a distinct twinge of regret.

'Pretty soon, yes. They've given me a lot of slack in this job, but I can't go on taking advantage. Though I think I may seriously consider going to uni. Not Durham though.'

'Too near to Juliet?'

'Precisely. I'm sorry, that sounds awful doesn't it? Selfish?'

'No, the right thing I think. It was always going to be different for you than it is for Juliet and Leo. Parents losing a son—that's not something they're ever going to get over.'

'Which is why I feel bad about wanting to get out of their lives, or at least wanting just to be another ordinary family friend. I guess if Luke hadn't died like that we very likely wouldn't still be together anyway. We were very young. It was nothing like the relationship you had with Miriam, nowhere near.'

'No.' He gazed at her. 'I shall miss you.'

'Oh, we must keep in touch, stay friends. That's not a problem.'

He grinned. 'I'm glad. Do you know, you're the first real friend I've made since Miriam died? It feels good, as if I've taken a step into normality.'

'Anyway, don't talk as if it's all over. Aren't we going to have a look at those records in Northamptonshire? It's the one thing we didn't do, find out about High Bagby.' High Bagby was a property mentioned in their lady's betrothal document as part of what she brought to the marriage. 'An awayday to Northampton!

I can't wait. But when?'

'Soon as ever we can. How about next Monday? Just to see if there are any records for High Bagby there, of the Machyn family. Or the Gaunts. Are you on for that then?'

'You bet! I'm not going to miss the last piece of the jigsaw.'

'We may not find anything more.'

'But then we'll know we haven't missed anything.' Then she hesitated. 'The only thing is, I think Juliet disapproves of our friendship.'

'But why? We're working on this for her, aren't we?'

'Of course. But I think she sees it as a betrayal of Luke for me to be friendly with anyone else. Oh, I know that's nonsense, and I expect she'd deny it if I challenged her. But I don't want to upset her if I can help it.'

'Is that a 'no' to coming with me to Northampton then?' He was clearly disappointed.

She shook her head. 'Never mind Juliet. I meant it when I said I wouldn't miss this for anything. But I'll have to try and let her down gently, be a model of tact.'

'Rosalind!'

Half way up the churchyard path on her

way to the Sunday Communion service, Rosalind turned and waited for Angela Wilkinson, head of Meadhope's primary school, to catch up with her.

'I meant to ring you about this.' She held out a piece of paper. 'Would you mind giving this out this morning? We want to get to as many people as possible.'

Rosalind glanced at the paper. *Memory afternoon*, she read. 'What is it?'

'We want older people to come into school and tell us about what it was like when they were kids—school, home, Christmas, wartime memories—give our students a taste of a different world. Help them realise that even old people were young once.'

'Sounds a lovely idea. Is this what Michelle was telling me about?' She glanced at the paper again, reading it through this time. 'Oh, not quite!'

'We decided to widen the remit. I think we can all learn a lot from it.'

'That's fine! I'll be happy to read it out.'

Returning after the service to the good cooking smells of the rectory, she made her way to where Alastair was in the kitchen. He turned to her with a look of excitement in his eyes. 'You'll never guess what I found, when I went to pick Mother up for church.'

'Don't tell me—she's got an army of carers waiting on her and a stair lift installed on her stairs!'

'You knew then? About the stair lift anyway?' There was no matching irony in Alastair's tone.

'I was joking—' Realisation crept into her mind. 'You're not serious?' Alastair beamed at her. 'So she's really given in at last? How wonderful!'

'She says it was to stop Josh worrying. So don't say anything. Leave her pride intact!'

'Of course. But when was it all done? Who organised it? They must have been incredibly speedy!'

'We have Josh to thank, I think.'

'In the middle of all his research too! He's really come to life hasn't he?'

'Indeed he has.' They shared smiles of relief and joy.

So eager was she to see this miracle, that Rosalind was tempted to offer to run Jessie home after lunch, but she knew her mother-in-law would much prefer to have her son or grandson as driver, so she allowed Josh to go instead.

As he drove away from the rectory, his

grandmother said casually. 'I think I might go along to that thing at the school.'

'What thing's that, Gran?'

'The thing in the notice your mother read out this morning. About asking older people to come and talk to the children.'

'What a good idea! I'm sure you'd enjoy it.'

'We older people have a great deal to teach the young, if they would only listen.'

'Well, they should be listening this time, if the teachers are there.'

Later, he told his parents of Jessie's decision. 'Goodness me!' exclaimed Rosalind. 'She's certainly got the wind in her sails these days! Amazing!'

'Do you think she'll cope all right, in her state of health?' Alastair looked anxious. 'I know she hasn't had any more attacks since they put her on that new medication, but still.'

'I suggested she asked Nurse Hutchinson to go along with her, but I don't think she fancied that.'

'Probably thought Phyllis would steal her thunder,' observed Alastair.

'I guess so. But if I'm around on Friday I'll go with her. Just hang about out of the way, just in case.'

Rosalind hugged him. 'You're a model

grandson, Josh.'

'Great! Any chance of a lift to the station tomorrow morning?'

Chapter Fifteen

It had been a difficult day for Juliet. Leo had insisted she help with installing the massive antique door he had found at last in a reclamation yard in a distant part of Northumberland. She'd approached the task with dread, which was tempered only by the fact that Katie offered willing help, and seemed completely untroubled by the sense of terror and reluctance that had crawled over Juliet's skin, set her scalp tingling, her throat tightening, from the moment Leo had mentioned the project.

'It's going to look amazing!' was Katie's verdict as she glanced from the door propped against the wall to the opening beside it, from which Leo was clearing the polythene sheeting. As Juliet felt the chill emerge from the stairwell, wrap her round, seep into her bones, Katie was running her hand appreciatively over the carving of the archway. 'Isn't it beautiful?'

Juliet did as she was asked, supporting the door, steadying it, while taking in little of the talk between Leo and their guest. She just wanted to get it over with, as soon as possible. She was thankful when enough time had passed for her to offer to make coffee for them all, and then lunch, after which her help was no longer needed. Katie lingered to watch Leo at work for a long time afterwards, so that by the evening she was in a rush to sort out her belongings for the next day's trip, before having an early night. Katie's visit was not proving the tranquil respite that Juliet had hoped for, in any sense.

As usual Juliet put off going to bed for as long as possible. She tried to write a letter to Celia, offering the forgiveness her old friend had asked for, but the words would not take shape, or not in any way that satisfied her. Instead, she settled down to read the two gardening books that had arrived from Amazon the previous day, but she was too weary to make much sense of them. In the end, she took Tiger with her and went reluctantly to bed. She allowed the animal to sleep in her arms; and soon, lulled by the soft warmth and the rhythmic purring, fell asleep herself.

Fear jarred her awake. Fear at her heart….No, not fear but terror, utter naked terror, not for herself, but for her son, her darling young son, so innocent of the world and its ways, so trusting; the son she should have protected, kept safe from harm, but instead had allowed to walk straight into the greatest peril of his life…

What could she do? How could she keep him safe, snatch him from danger? She lay there with fear churning in her stomach, the questions going round and round in her head without answers.

She opened her eyes and gazed at the flickering candle flame. She knew she ought to blow it out—fire was always a danger—but she was reluctant to give herself up to the darkness, to the intensified terrors that lurked in its shadows; the gentle light did not keep fear away, but held back the worst of it. Then, beyond it, her eyes fell on the carved wood of the prie dieu, the prayer desk, and she knew what she must do. She slipped from the bed, pulled her robe around her and knelt there before the painted figure of mother and child, the mother who had felt the sword of bitter pain pierce her maternal heart, who knew the greatest torment any mother could know. 'Sancta Maria, Mater Dei, ora pro nobis…'

By the time the first dawn light had begun to steal into the room, her limbs were aching more than usual, her fingers on the beads of the rosary were white with cold, but her mind was fixed on what she had to do, what she had to face today. And what the cost would be. By evening she would know if there was any room left for hope…

There was nothing she could do, no hope of putting things right. There in the grey dawn lighting the familiar twentieth century adornments of the room, that inescapable fact faced her in all its starkness: Luke had driven off into disaster, out of her life, out of all life, leaving only the ashes dispersed on the sea, the shattered lives of those who had loved him, who loved him still. There was no way back for them.

Juliet pulled the duvet close around her, exhausted, terrified, but fighting sleep, because sleep brought the risk of possession by the alien spirit, the woman who was not her, bringing the sickening loss of self, the obliteration of everything that made her what she was. She shrank from the possibility that it might happen again, the creeping certainty that it would, the dread that she might find there was no way back...Yet she longed for sleep, a deep untroubled dreamless sleep that might bring her refreshment and restoration, while knowing that there was no way into that sleep today, no peace to be found. Only pain, not just her pain, but the pain of the woman who had lived here once and left her grief embedded in the very fabric of the place, a grief that now was becoming, horribly, a part of her, flesh of her flesh, bone of her bone, linked inextricably to her own sense of loss.

She lay motionless for a long time, trying to calm herself as the light grew, but only feeling more shaken by grief than ever, clutched still by the horror of the night. It was bad enough to carry her own grief with her always, but to be invaded by another's, to find her dreams, once the only refuge she had from pain, taken over by this alien agony—that was beyond bearing.

She got up and went to have a shower, hoping to wash away some of the debris of the night. But it didn't work. Feeling no better, she dragged on her clothes, weary, limp with exhaustion. What now? How to escape all this? Would the research Katie and Josh were doing make any difference? How could it? If she were to know the story of this woman who haunted her, would that make her go away, or make the pain go away? Or would she have to leave Holywell to escape? She was beginning to fear that might be the only way out.

The kitchen was empty. She desperately wanted someone to talk to—even Leo would do. But she'd had that clear sense as she descended the stairs that she was alone in the house. Josh had been due to collect Katie at seven thirty, she recalled, for their day trip to wherever it was. But Leo too had gone out, for he'd left a note propped against the marmalade pot. *'Gone to York. Back for supper.'* She recalled dimly that he'd mentioned some firm in York run by—A friend? A former colleague?—which had asked for his advice, and would pay for it. Too good an opportunity to miss, he'd said, a way to keep his hand in, though he no longer had any enthusiasm for the accountancy work that had once been so great a part of his life.

She made herself some coffee, and then, after one sip, revolted by the very look of it, poured it down the sink and made blackcurrant tea instead, with a slice of toast that she only half ate. She felt weary, on edge, frazzled—and frightened. She desperately wanted company, any sort of ordinary human company. The silence seemed to grow and grow, taking on an almost tangible form, as if it were shouting at her.

I've got to go out, she thought. There was the garden, but it was shrouded in mist and today seemed in some way to have become an alien place, not the sanctuary it had always been before. She was completely unable to rediscover the old sense of being utterly at home there. She'd told Leo she would be working on the design for the dining room today, so that was something she'd better do, having no good excuse—or inclination—to do anything else. She went up to her study and put a Roberta Flack CD on the player and sat down with her sketch pad in front of her, and the sheaf of unsatisfactory possibilities she had already sketched. But though she put lines on the paper, rubbed out, started again, nothing useful emerged. All her creativity seemed to have dried up.

The day dragged along, hour by slow hour, without her knowing quite how or what she did to fill the time. She did force herself to spend a short while in the garden, but still it failed to work its charms on her and she soon gave up. She made herself a sandwich for lunch and ate half of it. After that, it seemed to grow dark very quickly—and then at last, earlier than she had feared, she heard the sound of Leo's car in the yard. She went out to meet him. He had a harassed look, as he used to long ago when returning from work in the city. He put his briefcase down in the passageway and hung up his coat, then coming into the kitchen he said in that old tense, weary voice, 'I need a whisky!' He went to the dresser and poured a large measure into a glass, with which he gestured towards her. 'You too?'

'No.' Something in her tone must have caught his attention through his exhaustion, for he turned to focus fully on her. 'You look terrible.'

'Thank you!' She came towards him. 'I will have that whisky after all.' She snatched the bottle from him and poured it herself. 'I don't think I can go on.' She tried to speak calmly but the stress of the day—and the night before—

brought her close to tears.

Alarmed, he took her arm and steered her towards a chair. 'Let's sit down and talk about this.' He sat down beside her. 'Now, what do you mean, you can't go on?'

'Living here.' She felt as though the words choked her.

'I thought you loved it. We both do. That was the whole point of coming here!'

'I didn't know then—what…It's what's in the house. I thought I could live with it, that it would go away, but it hasn't. It's getting worse.'

She heard his muffled exasperation. 'Oh for goodness sake, Juliet! Not that again. So you've been hearing more noises? It's not the house, it's you! Get that into your head!' He sighed, as if trying to be patient, and went on more calmly, 'Tell you what, why don't you go up to London for a few days, look up some old friends, do a bit of shopping; and make an appointment with that woman—I forget her name—the therapist you had recommended when— Well, the one you didn't go to see last year. I guess if you had we'd not be going through all this fanciful stuff now.'

She pushed back her chair, stood up, banged her hands on the table so hard that they hurt. 'Why can't you see? It's *not* fanciful stuff! It's *not* my imagination! I'm *not* going mad! This is really, actually happening! It's in the house, in the walls, down those stairs, coming in that door you opened up!'

'Oh, what nonsense! Anyway, I thought you found putting earplugs in kept the noises out?'

'Not any more,' she whispered. 'Now they— *she*—comes into my sleep.'

'You mean you dream about some ghostly woman?'

'No.' She found it hard to find the words to describe what had happened. 'It's not a dream, Leo. It's as if I'm being possessed, taken over. It's not my body any more. It's hers; and her mind, her thoughts. It's horrible.'

'Exactly. Nightmares *are* horrible.'

'I know it's not just a nightmare. I open my eyes, I'm awake, but what I see is all seen with her eyes, all around, the room, the furniture, everything. And I feel what she's feeling.'

'Who's this 'she', for goodness sake?'

'A woman who lived here once. Josh and Katie have been finding out about her. Everything they've found so far confirms what I've seen and heard.'

He looked a little relieved. 'And what they've found out has become part of your dreams! There, that's the simple explanation! That, and your own feelings, which you've transposed onto this imaginary woman.' He put an arm about her. 'Juliet, darling, you're sick, truly that's what it is—not mad, just troubled, understandably so! Things like this just don't happen, believe me. I'm not belittling it, but you need help, real skilled help from someone who's trained in such things.'

She shook him off and stepped back, away from him. 'Why can't you accept what I tell you? I *know* it's not in my mind! I know it's real! As real as you sitting there so smugly, refusing to hear what I say, not even trying to understand! Don't you think I'd much rather it was just in my head? I could deal with bad dreams, but not this, not this—' She was close to tears. 'I just want things to get back to normal.' Normal: life without Luke, the emptiness of all that—? No, what she really wanted was to go back to life as it once had been, with hope, with a future, not this life that consisted only of *now*, and beyond it the rolling fog of the dreary unknown years of ageing. She stood by the table with tears running down her cheeks, longing for understanding and sympathy, real sympathy, while Leo simply stood there watching her with an expression of cold distaste. 'I just want you to understand!'

'Oh, but I do understand! Why else do I keep telling you to get some help? I've been telling you since the first time you said you heard noises. Your trouble is—' His voice slowed, cautious, choosing the words with care: 'You've never dealt with your grief. That's at the root of it.'

'But it's not just me! Josh Maclaren heard the noises too, that first time he was here—sobbing, just like I heard. How do you explain that away?'

His explanation was precisely as she had predicted to Josh at the time. 'He's got problems of his own, from what I gather.'

She felt rather as if she were staring not at Leo's obstinate expression, but at a gleaming wall of impenetrable marble, on which she could make no impression, no matter how hard she tried. 'So anyone who's lost someone is going to hear strange noises in the night? Is that what you're saying? Then why haven't you heard things too?'

'Because I'm a rational being. Because I've come to terms with what happened.'

'Come to terms! How have you ever come to terms? When? You've never once talked about it in all the months since it happened, not to me, not to anyone else, as far as I know!'

He stood there, facing her, calm, imperturbable, sure of his rightness. 'I have dealt with it in my own way. It's happened, it's over. I've moved on. You need to do the same.'

'How can you ever move on from the loss of a child? It's against nature, against everything that life ought to be! You can't just shrug it off as if it was the death of a pet cat or something! And you—you've never looked it in the face, never admitted what really happened. Dear Lord, it was your doing, your fault, and you behave as if you can carry on as if nothing had changed! Well, I can't, I just can't, and I don't understand how you possibly can, unless you're the most cold and heartless person who ever lived!'

The only alteration in his expression was an increasing tightness about the lips, which constricted his voice, subduing to a harsh whisper the fierce anger of its undertow. 'Don't you think I regret every day of my life that I ever bought him that car? Damn you, Juliet, damn you for even suggesting that I don't feel it! But we can't go back—we can't bring him back. He's dead—dead and gone! That's it. Final. This is all we have left. Deal with it. And get over this stupid fantasy about a ghost.'

Such a cold face, so adamant, so sure he was

right, so heedless of her pain, impervious to it—why had she stayed with him for so long? How could she ever have thought there was hope for them, a future for their marriage?

Something inside her suddenly broke. All the long months of restraint, the agony unshared, the anger that had seethed inside her, were wrenched from her in an explosion of sobbing. Seized by rage she launched herself at him, pummelling his chest with her fists. 'I hate you, Leo! I hate you! I can never forgive you for what you did, never! I begged and begged you not to get that car, not even to promise it, but you wouldn't listen, wouldn't even have the sense to get a cheap old thing, something slow and boring! You wouldn't listen, you had it stuck in your vain stubborn head, it had to be the most powerful car you could find, just what any boy racer would die for—and he did die. Just so you could show everyone what a wonderful father you were! But it didn't did it? You killed our son as surely as if you'd pointed a gun at his head! You're nothing better than a murderer! Murderer! Murderer! Murderer—!' Vision clouded with tears, she dropped onto the floor and lay huddled there like a child, sobbing beyond control.

'Stop it! Shut up! You're hysterical!'

She felt his hands on her shoulders, pulling at her, and with a great effort threw him off. 'Don't touch me! Don't ever touch me again, ever!' She sat back on her heels, her face streaked with tears, her expression implacable. Her voice now was rough, faint, cold. 'It's over, Leo. I was a fool to think anything else. You killed our son. There's no future for us after that, there never was, never could be, never.'

He stared down at her, his face drained of colour. 'Well, now we have the truth—what you really think of me! God, woman, is this what's been in your head all this time? No wonder you have bad dreams! Well, don't worry—I'll not ask you to go on living with a murderer!'

It was some time before she realised he had left the room; still longer before, as she calmed a little, she heard the slam of the door and—soon after—the sound of his car driving away.

It was very quiet. She couldn't even hear the wind, or the whoosh of the Aga as it fired up, or the hum of the fridge, or the tiny clicking noises a house makes as it adjusts to the closing in of the night. Limp with exhaustion, she made her way to the sitting room and sank down on the sofa. She wished there was a fire in here, but she hadn't the energy to light one. Perhaps she should go to bed—but then Katie would be back soon, and it would be good to have someone to talk to. She gave a bitter inward smile. *What have I got to talk about? How Leo's gone and our marriage is almost certainly at an end, and I don't know what I'm going to do? How I can't take any more, can't live here any more, but have nowhere else to go, nowhere I want to go, nothing I want to do?* Some time those things would have to be faced, but not yet, not tonight, not now. It was far too soon and she had no words left. Besides, if she were to confide in anyone, it would not be Katie, who had so disappointed her.

The silence seemed to grow around her, almost as if it were taking physical shape, becoming not a state but a presence. It was not in any sense a peaceful silence. It was like the lull before a storm, she thought, in that moment just as it was about to break; and then told herself she was being fanciful.

Without a fire the chill of the room soon reached her. It was already ten o'clock. *Never mind Katie, I'm going to bed*, she decided. She called Tiger, who usually answered to his name, but he didn't come. Having failed to find him anywhere in the house, she opened the back door and peered out into the yard, calling and calling. She glimpsed him by the stile that led into the trees beyond the yard, but he didn't move, just sat there. She went towards him, but he bounded away into the darkness. 'I'm not in the mood for games!' she told him, but she knew he was too far off to hear—and even if he wasn't, he clearly had no intention of coming in. He would make his way home in his own good time, through the cat flap they'd had fitted; which meant she must go to bed without him.

She went upstairs, wishing there was someone else in the house, a living breathing human being, even Leo—even Leo livid with rage as he'd been when he'd walked out of the door. She'd told him it was over, but she knew now she hadn't meant it, didn't even want it. But it was too late to take back the words. He had gone.

As she reached each room, each passage and hallway, she switched on all the lights she could, central lights, wall lights and every table, standard and desk lamp that lit the darker corners. She did not switch them off again as she moved from passage to stairs, crossed the landing and went into her own room, closing the door behind her as soon as every light in there was switched on too.

She had a quick hot shower—wishing as she did so that her thoughts did not drift inexorably to that ineradicable scene from Hitchcock's

Psycho—towelled herself vigorously dry, put on her nightdress and slipped into bed. Tonight she would sleep with the light on—if she slept at all. For now, she was going to read, a soothing familiar friend of a book of the kind she kept always beside her bed in case she needed to calm herself. Lately it had been *The Secret Garden* —after all, didn't she have a secret garden of her own?

That was it, that was what she must allow to fill her mind, thoughts about the garden as it had been always until today, her haven, her retreat! She opened the book at the postcard of Hidcote gardens that she was using as a bookmark, and picked up the story at the first meeting between Dickon and Mary. Soon the lovely familiar words had closed round her, exhaustion giving gradual way to sleepiness.

Perhaps she slept; she had no idea. What she did know was that she found herself somehow in that other place, the room that was hers and not hers. She had become the person that was herself and not herself, and was gazing out at the flickering firelight, the guttering candle flame, the bed hangings that stirred in the draught from ill-fitting windows.

Heavy silence pressed down on the room, the silence that was an actual presence—a presence that was gathering its forces together, strengthening, building round her. Her heart thudded, her throat tightened and dried, she felt a chill crawl up her spine.

Like a wave poised to break, everything went absolutely still, motionless. Nothing stirred. The candle flame simply went out, as if an unseen hand had snuffed it, the fire died down to a faint distant glow. She clutched the side of the bed, bracing herself, waiting—for what?

It burst over the room with a thunderous roar, rushing through the windows, swirling about her, wrapping her round, filling her to the brim with terror and despair and bitter grief. The air was full of cries, far off and near; a stench came with it, of putrefaction, of rotting flesh. She felt herself retch.

She had a sudden, horrible fugitive glimpse of a human shape, covered with heavy black cloth, a human who was no longer human, a corpse...

Then she was swept up in a storm of sound, sobbing, screaming, banging, rattling on windows, a storm blowing outside and inside— inside the house, inside her body, inside her head. There was no escape from it, no way out. She no longer knew who she was, what she was. She pressed her hands to her face, but still she saw everything—what did she see? She saw the ancient doorway, the door flung suddenly wide, swinging on its hinges; the spiral staircase filled with clattering feet, grotesque shadows, coming up and up, towards this place. Noise battered her, growing, overwhelming. The bedroom door swung open, a fierce bitter stinking wind howled in, swirled about, gathering up everything in its path. A chair fell over, and the prie dieu; the hangings were dragged from the bed as if unseen hands pulled them. Now they seemed to clutch at her, those hands—

With a massive effort of will, a strength she did not know was in her, she tore herself from the bed and ran from the room. The wind and the noise went with her, the storm battered her, tugged at her clothes, trying to hold her back. It came at her from all sides, a turbulence that swept pictures from the walls—she heard the crash of broken glass—toppled furniture, a chair, a table. As she ran across the landing, she felt something fall so close it brushed her shoulder in the darkness. She had left lights on, but now there were none, no candles, no electric lamps, nothing, just a lurid gleam briefly glimpsed then gone as she felt her way down the stairs, along the passage, into the kitchen. She failed to find the light switch, stumbled over a fallen chair, felt something sharp, painful under her foot—broken glass? All around her unseen hands were gathering up crockery and glass, pots and pans, flinging them around in a hurricane of destruction. She must get to the door, out into the yard, away from here—! As she felt her way, limping from her cut foot, her hand closed on something that lay on the table, a leather tab, cold hard metal. Car keys. Her car keys.

The car! The car, now—that was it, that was what she must do! She felt her way, hands on the walls, along the passage, pushing against the force that tried to stop her, to drag her back to the rooms she had left; trying not to heed the things that battered her, flung around as if in the heart of a cyclone. At last she felt the door under her shaking hands, struggled with the bolts, got them free at last and pulled at the latch. Cold fresh air hit her. She ran across the yard to her car.

Jump in, slam doors, lock them, turn keys in the ignition. *Dogger, Fisher, German Bight…* The radio had been left on, and the calm narrative of the shipping forecast filled the space around her. She leaned back and closed her eyes. *Thank God! Thank God!*

She was bruised, shivering, soaking wet—it

must have been raining then…Yes, it was pouring, a fierce torrent that hammered on the car roof, streamed down the windows. She glanced towards the house, but could see nothing for the dark and the rain. All she knew was that she must escape, now, no matter where. She switched on the wipers, set the car in motion and drove away, barefoot, along the drive.

Where to? The car clock told her it was nearly one o'clock in the morning. A hotel perhaps—but she didn't want the anonymity of a hotel. Besides, she had no money, nothing, not even a coat. And even if she had those things, who knew what might await her there, alone in an unknown room, what might have followed? She needed someone, a friend…

Rosalind, who had said, *Any time you need me, day or night, I'll always be there for you.*

The rectory was in darkness when she ran from the car where she'd parked it in the lane, across the garden to the porch sheltering the front door. She hesitated just a moment and then pressed the bell, once, twice, three times; insistently.

A head appeared at an upper window—not Rosalind, a man: Alastair.

What am I doing? He'd be furious that his

sleep had been disturbed. In any case he hardly knew her. 'Rosie——!' she implored.

The head disappeared, lights came on, and then Rosalind was at the door and had her arms about her and was drawing her inside. 'You're soaked—and in your nightie! You must be frozen! And what's this on your face? Has someone been hitting you? Juliet, what's happened?'

What had happened? A dream? A nightmare? No, not that. A haunting? She had no idea. She tried to give some sort of explanation, but it sounded garbled, confused, utterly implausible. 'Never mind now,' Rosalind soothed her. 'Let's get you some dry clothes.'

'I'll go and make up the spare bed,' she heard Alastair say.

Rosalind found a pair of warm pyjamas, helped Juliet out of her wet nightdress and into the dry clothes. 'Now, a hot drink—in bed or downstairs?'

'Downstairs. I don't want to be alone.'

Chapter Sixteen

'I can't thank you enough.' Having demolished boiled eggs and toast, Juliet was sitting in the rectory kitchen with a mug of tea cradled in her hands. 'It all seems a bit foolish by the light of day. I'm sorry I caused you such a disturbed night.'

Before going to bed, she had told Rosalind as much as she could bear of what had happened, though it all seemed rather vague and intangible in the telling, like clutching at smoke. But it was not quite true that, in the light of a bright morning, it all seemed 'a bit foolish'. Even now, she felt as limp and exhausted as if she had been battered by an actual storm, and the terror of what she had been through still lingered just below the surface; but she hoped that by belittling it she might come to believe it had been insignificant and trivial, exaggerated in her imagination. Only the row with Leo, and his going, were concrete things she could speak of in a normal way—along with the other thing that angered and hurt her: 'Katie didn't come back,' she'd told Rosalind last night, wondering if she were here all the time, in bed with Josh.

'Didn't she ring you? Oh, that's too bad of her! Josh called yesterday evening to say they were following up something they'd found and would be staying away another night. I'm surprised she didn't let you know.' But then Rosalind wasn't aware of how awkward their relationship had become lately.

After that, Juliet had at last felt able to go to bed, where she'd slept soundly, dreamlessly, until well into the morning. Rosalind had found her a sweater and jeans that fitted her well enough—they were much of a size—though she was conscious that her hair looked a mess, not having had the help of her usual hair products after her shower (Rosalind did not bother with such things, whether from lack of vanity or because her fiery curls were beyond the aid of anything but a brush and comb).

'What now? Are you ready to go home? You're welcome here as long as you want—that goes without saying. Whatever you feel is best.'

Juliet shrank at the very thought of returning to Holywell. 'I guess you think it was all my imagination, don't you? There was an ordinary storm—'

'Josh heard things too, remember.'

'Yes…I should go back to feed Tiger. But—' She gazed earnestly at her friend. 'Rosie, does your church do exorcisms?'

'We don't call it that. But yes, the diocese has

what they call a deliverance team that we can turn to for advice or whatever.' She paused a moment; then went on, choosing her words with evident care, 'I should warn you. They do tend to investigate the possibility that there might be a psychological explanation for any manifestation.'

'You mean—they'll assume I'm just a hysterical woman? That I'm imagining it, that Leo's right—?'

'They'll not assume anything. Nor will they even suggest it's not very real. Just that it may not be a simple matter of haunting by a ghost, in the way most people think of such things. This isn't a horror film. It's real life.'

'So you think it's all in my mind—you as well?' The hurt showed in her eyes. 'I thought you of all people believed me!'

'Of course I do.' She held Juliet's hands in hers. 'Listen, that's not what I'm saying, not at all. But it might be that you are picking up something that's already there because you're grieving. Perhaps that's why Josh heard things too.'

'So Leo can't be grieving because he doesn't hear anything?' That was precisely what she had accused him of, yet now she felt herself repudiate the very idea.

'Not at all. He's just a different person. Or I'd guess that's it. I don't know. I'm not an expert, if there is such a thing in matters like this. I just wanted to warn you what to expect.'

'I think you're telling me that they're not actually likely to do anything, except talk to me and tell me it's going to be all right?' She sounded bitter, let down.

'They'll do something concrete, I'm sure— or advise me how to deal with it. Sometimes they do carry out what amounts to exorcism. No bell, book and candle though. Mostly prayer.'

'Does it work?'

'I've no experience of it either way. But, yes, I think it usually helps. Would you like me to contact them?'

'I think so.' Her mind went back to the terror of the night, shrank at the thought of returning to Holywell. 'Yes, I would. Yes please.'

'And your cat—I'll drive over and feed him, if you like—'

She was interrupted by a sudden wild ring of the doorbell, accompanied by a frantic hammering on the door. 'What is it with everyone at the moment?' Alastair raised his eyes in mock exasperation as he went to answer it.

Leo stumbled over the doorstep. 'Is Juliet

here? It was the only place——'

'She's here, safe and well. Come on in.'

'Thank God for that!' He followed Alastair to the sitting room. 'There was no one at the house. The door was open and everything blown around in the kitchen——must have been open all through that storm——and no sign of her, only lights left on everywhere. I couldn't think where she might be, then——'

He saw Juliet, ran to her and pulled her into his arms. 'Oh thank God you're safe!'

She stiffened, hesitated for just a moment, and then fell against him, clinging to him, shaken by wrenching sobs. Rosalind got up, touched Alastair's arm, and together they left the room, closing the door behind them.

'You'd better tell me what happened,' Leo said at last. 'And how you got those bruises on your face.'

She pulled away from him. 'You'll say I imagined it.'

'Not this time. I promise.' He hugged her closer. 'There was a bad feeling about the place this morning. Even I could sense it. And Tiger too——that was the clincher.'

'Oh, is he all right? He hasn't been fed.'

'He has now, don't worry. I found him cowering in the yard, all soaking wet, so I picked him up and tried to carry him indoors—but he bit and scratched like a wild thing and then ran off. There was no way he was going into that house. So I took his food out to that tumbledown shed by the field gate and he seemed all right there. That did convince me though—whatever happened in the house last night, it scared that cat silly. And cats don't suffer from too much imagination as far as I know. So you'd better tell me what it was.'

She told him, adding what Rosalind had said about the part her emotional state might have played. For the first time he listened to her account of what he would once have dismissed as delusion in a sympathetic silence, stroking her hair, making consoling murmurs whenever she paused in her narrative. At the end, he simply held her, his face bent against the top of her head. 'I haven't helped, have I? And yesterday —I'm sorry. I was angry. But with myself, not you. What happened to Luke—well, you know! It's hard to live with, but I have to, there's no choice. For me anyway. The question is, can you live with it—can you live with me? Yesterday you said you couldn't.'

She gazed at him, considering. It was all she'd wanted from him, to admit his part in the loss of their son. All these months her rage had festered, eating away at her. That was what had come between them, prevented any intimacy, any meeting of minds; kept them from sharing their grief and finding comfort from one another. But it had been a part of her so long— could she now move on from it so easily, leave it behind? Could she even forgive?

What was there to forgive? A moment of indulgent thoughtlessness that had led to catastrophe? If Leo had for one moment guessed what might happen, he would never have done it, of course he wouldn't. Very probably he would never be able to forgive himself for it as long as he lived. But could she?

She gave a watery smile. 'I can try. I want to try. That's all I can promise for now.'

'It'll have to do.' He kissed her. 'Thank you. Now, what are we going to do about the house? Sell up and cut our losses?'

If he'd asked her last night, fresh from the horror of what had happened, she would have said yes at once. Now she was astonished at the strength of her repudiation of the very thought of leaving Holywell. It had brought her terror, and at the moment she shrank from the prospect of returning there. Yet—it was already a part of her. She was bound up with it, with the woman who haunted her, the garden, the long years of its history. It was her future—their future. It was unfinished business.

'No. I want to stay—I want us to stay. On one condition—so long as what happened…so long as nothing like that happens again, ever, that it's all over. So—I'd like Rosalind to arrange some sort of exorcism—I know you're going to say that's nonsense,' she added quickly, before he could respond.

'If it makes you feel better, that's all right with me. You can bring in bell, book and candle, the lot. Just don't ask me to take part, that's all!' Then, 'Now, do we go home, back to Holywell, or do you want to stay here for the time being? If we go back, I'll come in with you tonight, to our bed.'

She gave a shaky laugh. 'Your snoring should keep the ghosts away!' Then she hesitated, abruptly silent, before adding soberly, 'Let's go back, now, and I'll see how I feel, how it feels to me. I doubt if I'm going to want to stay there at night, not yet anyway. But I'm sure Rosalind will let me use her spare bed for a bit longer if need be.'

As the car came within sight of Holywell, Juliet felt the knot tighten in her stomach, her mouth dry. Leo glanced at her. 'All right?'

'Yes,' she said, though she was by no means sure of it.

He drove into the yard and parked, giving her a brief hug. 'Courage, my dear!'

As they got out of the car Katie came to meet them, Josh a few paces behind. 'What's been happening here? Are you all right?'

Suddenly glad to see her, yet feeling shaken still, Juliet kissed her. 'I'm fine.' Behind her, Leo asked,

'How did you two get here?'

'Someone I know was at the station,' said Josh. 'Gave us a lift. We thought you'd be here.'

'We are now. Explanations can wait.'

They went into the house, where Katie said, 'We've been doing a bit of tidying up, I hope you don't mind. Something weird's been going on—even the kitten won't come indoors. It looked as if a whirlwind had hit it. The house I mean.'

'That's about it,' said Juliet with a tremulous smile. She felt as if a layer of skin had been torn from her, as if every nerve was stretched, braced for another assault.

Yet it was all so normal, so comforting: Katie putting on the kettle, Leo hunting in the cupboard for biscuits, Josh finding mugs to put ready on the table—which was not so easy, for many of them had gone, found smashed on the floor, though the debris had mostly been cleared away by now. Juliet sat down, not even offering to help.

'I've asked Ros—your mother—to see about exorcism. Or whatever they call it.'

The two young people stopped what they were doing and stared at her. 'Oh!' Katie came to sit opposite her.

'You don't want us to do that!' Juliet realised with surprise.

'I don't know,' said Katie.

'That depends—' said Josh. 'I think we've found out as much as there is to know. Do you want to hear it?'

Over tea and biscuits, they told her. This time, Leo listened as attentively as did his wife.

'She was called Katharine Machyn, the woman who lived here in the early seventeenth century. We think she moved here after her husband died, probably with her children. As we thought she seems to have been a Catholic, at a time when you were penalised for being one. Her family were involved in the Gunpowder plot.'

'Ah!' said Leo. 'Guy Fawkes—the only man ever to enter Parliament with honest intentions!' He gave a rueful grin at their laughter. 'Sorry—

very old joke that. And it looks a bit different these days. I guess they were terrorists in today's terms.'

'Absolutely!' agreed Katie. 'Once they'd destroyed the government, they planned to set up a puppet Catholic state and force everyone to turn Catholic too. They were complete fanatics. Even if they'd succeeded I guess most Catholics would have been appalled by what they'd done. As it was, it just made life much harder for them. After the Gunpowder plot Catholics in England must have felt a bit like I guess some Muslims do today, demonised.' She grinned sheepishly. 'Sorry—didn't mean to give you a history lecture! Let's get back to Katharine Machyn. Go on, Josh.'

'Yes, well, anyway, it seems this place called High Bagby, which doesn't exist any more— that's where she was when she married. It was part of her dowry. Well, it was just a mile or so from Ashby St Ledgers, which belonged to Robert Catesby, the leading plotter. We guess the two families would be close, being Catholics and neighbours. Her husband's place at Haroby was not so far away either—quite a network of Catholics in that area. Anyway, she had a brother—Nicholas Gaunt, he was called. He worked for Catesby and was up to his neck in the plot. We think one of her sons may once have worked for Catesby too—he was taken in for questioning, though we don't know if anything happened to him. It looks as though her brother escaped, probably fled abroad, maybe the only one of the plotters who did.'

Clear into Juliet's mind came a vision of the shrouded corpse glimpsed at the heart of the horror…She felt an icy chill along her spine, fear clutch at her stomach. 'No—he didn't,' she heard herself say. 'He died. I'm certain of it. I don't know how or why; I just know.' She caught Josh's startled look and forced a faint smile. 'I know that sounds ridiculous. But then this whole thing is, isn't it? If you look at it rationally, that is.' She glanced at Leo, and saw scepticism in his eyes, but nothing worse; he even gave a half-smile.

'Don't expect me to disagree with that last remark,' he said. 'All I can admit is that something happened here last night.'

'I think her fear and her grief, for her son and her brother—I think they've left a mark on the house. Maybe there's guilt too. In fact, thinking about it, she could have betrayed him to the authorities. She'd have her children to think of, and they'd come first. I don't know. What I am sure of is that something very painful happened that's stopping her from resting. And that's why I want your mother, Josh, to do something to try and bring peace— because I think that if all the guilt and grief or whatever it is are wiped out then all that will remain is her love of this place, and that's a good thing.'

'And if it doesn't work?'

'I don't know.'

'Time you stopped for lunch,' declared Alastair at the rectory, putting his head round the study door.

'There's soup in the pan if you're hungry.'

'Only if you'll join me.' Reluctantly, Rosalind agreed. As they sat together in the kitchen, he asked, 'Have you had any word from Juliet, to say how she's getting on?'

'I spoke to her just now. She's all right. A bit shaky still, though she seems to be coping. But I think she'll be coming back here overnight.'

'If it was me I'd want to move out altogether.'

'You don't think it's nonsense then? Or her imagination?'

'Why—do you?'

'No, not at all. Though I guess her emotional state has stirred something up that was already there. After all, if you really think about it, it's not so strange if people who've lived in a place, the emotions they've gone through, should leave their mark somehow. In every other way they leave traces, where they've altered the place, even where they've touched things or walked on them. A drop of blood on an oak floor will stay there for centuries—don't you remember that stately home we went to once, where they showed us the stain? So why not emotions too, joy and guilt and grief?'

'So are you going to do this exorcism thing?'

'That's what I've been doing this morning— talking to someone from the deliverance team.'

'Will they come?'

'They don't think they need to at this stage.'

'Oh. What does that mean? That you've got to do it?'

'It'll be a matter of prayers and holy water, something very simple and low key. Not much more than blessing the house, like I did when the Palmers moved into their new place and asked me to bless it. I've told Juliet I'll come over the day after tomorrow, first thing.'

'Do you really believe it will work?'

'I don't know. I've never done anything quite like this before. If it doesn't, then I'll hand over to someone else. But hopefully it will.' She smiled. 'It's not in my hands, is it?'

Alastair looked at her intently. 'Are you scared?'

'Should I be?'

'It's obvious there's something's going on there. Some people would say you're meddling with dark forces.' There was a note of mock terror in his voice, which made Rosalind smile.

'You've been watching too many horror films. I don't see this as a battle with Satan, you know. More a kind of spring clean.'

Alastair laughed. 'How very Anglican!'

She put her arm about him. 'Are you terribly disappointed?'

'Desolated!' He kissed her. 'You take care, mind! You never know.'

She drew back then, her expression grave. 'There is one thing I am afraid of, to be honest.' She had his complete attention. 'If it doesn't work. If it has no effect. What then? Does that mean I'm quite wrong, that there is such a thing as the devil, that evil can have a tangible shape, that it needs more than earnest heartfelt prayers to combat it?'

'But you do believe there is such a thing as evil.'

'Yes—but not quite like that. Not as a kind of equal force to good; to God.'

Alastair held her in his arms. 'Do you want me to come with you?'

'No—no, I don't think so. Just be ready to pick up the pieces afterwards!'

'You know I always am.'

Chapter Seventeen

It was going to be a fine day, though the sun had not yet broken through the early mist as Rosalind turned into the drive that led to Holywell. Juliet, beside her, said, 'It looks so beautiful. So peaceful.' She had stayed at the rectory each night since her flight from the house, and she and Rosalind had spent several hours discussing what was going to be done this morning. Josh, in the car as well, had joined in too.

'It *will* be peaceful again,' Rosalind reassured her with a confidence she did not wholly feel. But then, as she'd said to Alastair, the outcome did not depend on her alone.

Tiger came bounding up to Juliet as she got out of the car, but though he twined himself, purring, about her legs all the way to the house door where Leo and Katie waited, he would not pass through it with her. 'That'll be the test of the efficacy of your incantations,' Leo said to Rosalind; 'if this animal dares to come inside again.'

Rosalind, carrying a case with the things she needed, followed him through the rooms, Juliet, increasingly reluctant, behind her.

'I've put everything ready in the hall, as you

asked.' He turned to grin at her. 'It all feels very odd to me. A bit hocus pocus.'

'Let's see, shall we?' Rosalind's tone was grave, quiet. She seemed distant, as if absorbed in what she was doing, far from trivial considerations.

The hall had a distinct chill about it, but as far as Rosalind was concerned it was the ordinary everyday chill of an unheated room with ancient stone walls. Juliet hung back in the doorway, as if poised for flight. She watched as Rosalind went to the folding garden table Leo had erected in the middle of the room, placing on it a candle from her case, which she lit. Katie and Josh took their seats on the garden chairs that formed a circle about the table, as did Leo, to Juliet's surprise. *'If it helps, that's fine by me. Just don't ask me to take part,'* he'd said when Juliet explained the arrangements that had been made. Now he turned towards her and held out his hand, his expression full of tenderness. She forced herself into the room, to the empty chair at his side, and felt his hand close about hers.

The oddness of it all distracted her, as she watched Rosalind discharge with quiet concentration the unfamiliar rituals of her office; the friend transmuted into the priest. Having handed each of them a sheet of paper with the words of various prayers printed on it, Rosalind took a flask of holy water from her case and poured some of its contents into a silver dish, which she placed on the table beside what looked for all the world like a small whisk —an aspergil, she had explained last night at the rectory. Then she unfolded her stole, the strip of heavy embroidered cloth that she wore when officiating at a service, bringing to her lips the cross that marked its exact centre, before putting it about her neck. She opened her book of prayers, took the last remaining seat, and made the sign of the cross. 'In the name of the Father and the Son and the Holy Spirit. Amen.

'Let's begin with the Lord's Prayer. *Our Father…*'

Juliet murmured the words—once so familiar, now a little uncertain from disuse— lulled by the soft sound of the united voices, with their ancient echoes, their memories of so many occasions, large and small: school assemblies, weddings; funerals—

'*Lead us not into temptation, but deliver us from evil…*' She felt a sudden chill, like an icy finger at the nape of her neck, and heard, faintly, far off, the sound of sobbing. Raising her head she saw in Josh's eyes, meeting hers, a recognition that he too had heard it. Then it was gone. The room was quiet again.

'A reading now, from psalm 91: we'll read alternate verses, I'll read the first, then you read the second together, and so on.

'Whoso dwelleth under the defence of the most High: shall abide under the shadow of the Almighty…

'He shall defend thee under his wings, and thou shalt be safe under his feathers…' Juliet smiled at the image of God as a mother hen; there was something comforting about it. But it was not enough, nowhere near enough, to drive the fear away.

'Thou shalt not be afraid for any terror by night: nor for the arrow that flieth by day…' Oh but she was, she was deadly afraid!

Rosalind rose, took up the bowl and aspergil, and moved towards the door that led to the spiral stair. 'We shall go together!'

They followed, Leo's arm supporting Juliet, steadying her trembling limbs.

Rosalind halted. *'Bring peace to this house, oh lord, and to all who dwell in it.'* She dipped the aspergil into the water and sprayed it against the door. Then she put her hand on the latch and pulled the door open. Juliet tried to call to her to stop, but her voice froze in her throat and she could say nothing.

'Lord Jesus Christ, who came to share in an earthly home at Nazareth, we ask you to enter this home and

bless it with your presence. Drive from it all evil, keep safe all those who dwell in it and bring them peace, that they may live together in harmony…' She sprayed more water.

*All who dwell in it…*past and present, held together in one prayer…

More holy water; a pause. Silence. The doorway gaped wide, shadowed, the worn steps leading upwards into darkness as Rosalind walked towards them.

'Bring peace to this house, oh lord…'

From somewhere in the dark beyond sight came a noise that was part roar, part scream; human, yet less than human. The rush of wind from the stairs was so fierce that Rosalind staggered back, dropping the water, the stole half-dragged from her shoulders.

Wind that was more than wind, a force that was some Thing—some *One*—swept into the room, gathering dust, dead leaves, grit, cobwebs into a stinking whirlwind. That stench again, the one from the night—Juliet recognised it as the prayer sheet was torn from her hands. It pulled at their clothes, set them reaching out for support as it swirled about them. Katie screamed; Rosalind, one hand on the wall, held the other towards them. 'Hold on!' They barely heard her above the noise, struggled to push against the wind, arms clutching one another's shoulders, huddling together, forming a protective circle at the heart of the tumult.

Rosalind began to sing words from the sheet, still in her hand. *'I bind unto myself today, the strong name of the Trinity...'* Her voice sounded faint, weak, ineffectual, lost in the roar of the wind. Then Josh joined in, and one by one the rest of them, struggling to read the words, find the tune, but slowly, gradually, gathering force. *'... His heavenly host to be my guard...*

'Christ be with me, Christ within me,
'Christ behind me, Christ before me...
'Christ beside me, Christ to win me,
'Christ to comfort and restore me,
'Christ beneath me, Christ above me,
'Christ in quiet, Christ in danger...'

Above their determined singing, the clamour grew, intensified. No longer just roaring and shrieking, but augmented by sounds like clattering hooves, murderous shouts, the crashing of angry fists, cudgels, iron bars on a heavy door. Circling round them, the Thing pressed against them, battered them, pushing them so close together they could scarcely breathe. They bent their heads, braced themselves, held on. Katie was sobbing with terror. They could no longer even try to sing. *It's over,* Juliet thought. *It's over.*

Rosalind's voice soared above the noise,

strong, confident, commanding: '*Visit this place, oh lord, we pray, and drive far from it the snares of the enemy; may your holy angels dwell with us and guard us in peace and may your blessing be always upon us; through Jesus Christ our Saviour.*' Her head was up now, her eyes gazing towards the doorway. She raised her hand to make the sign of the cross.

As her hand moved steadily down, firmly across, it was as if a heavy blanket had fallen on a fire, extinguishing it in one swift move. Silence filled the room; a hush so complete that their gasps for breath sounded raucous in the stillness.

Slowly, heads were raised. Josh steadied himself against the wall, then put his arm about Katie; she looked very white, but then so did he. Juliet felt Leo's arms about her, holding her, soothing her. Rosalind herself was visibly trembling.

She bent and retrieved the silver bowl, which still had a little water in it, so she sprayed more on the door and then went to top it up from the flask in her case, which was now at the far side of the room, against the wall where the table and chairs too lay in a tangled heap. She led them—unsteadily, warily—out of the hall, along the passage, through the further rooms, up the stairs, pausing in each doorway to sprinkle holy water and repeat the blessing. '*Visit this place, O Lord, we pray, and drive far from it the snares of the enemy; may your holy angels dwell with us and guard us in peace and may your blessing be always upon us; through Christ our Saviour. Amen.'* By the end, with every door lintel sprinkled, every room blessed, the tremor had gone from her voice and they were all murmuring the words with her.

At last she led them back to the hall, where they stood for the final prayers. *'May the Lord bless you and keep you, the Lord look upon you and be gracious to you, may the Lord lift up the light of his face upon you and give you his peace, now and always. Amen.*

'Now, let's hold hands and say the grace together:

'The blessing of God Almighty, Father, Son and Holy Spirit, be with us all, now and ever more. Amen.'

Quiet voices, a quiet room; they raised their heads and gazed at one another, each trying to make out what the others thought and felt.

Is this enough? wondered Juliet. *Is this really the end of it all?* She felt drained, exhausted, yet even so something seemed different about this room, some horror had fled from it, so that it now felt simply what it was, an ancient, beautiful hall. The door to the spiral stair was open still, yet she had no sense of terror when she glanced, warily, towards it. Would it last? Only time would tell.

As Rosalind put away her stole, gathered her things together, and Leo folded chairs and table,

Juliet said with forced cheerfulness, 'Coffee everyone?' The banality of the question fell into the room like a brick through the window, shocking them—eventually—into shaky laughter.

'I don't know about anyone else, but I need something a damn sight stronger than coffee!' retorted Leo.

They made their way to the kitchen, where the first thing Juliet saw was Tiger, curled up in the warmest spot beside the Aga, fast asleep. 'Well, he thinks it's all right,' she said, and turned to smile her gratitude to Rosalind.

As his mother drove the two of them back to Meadhope, Josh said, 'Mum, what the hell was going on in there?'

'I don't know, to be honest. I'm not sure. But it wasn't at all what I expected. Not that I knew what to expect exactly.'

'It was scary, very scary. I thought—Well—'

'You thought it wasn't going to work?

'Yes. Then—when you said that prayer, at the end, you sounded different somehow. Not like you.'

'It wasn't me. The words came, that's all.'

He gave a shaky laugh. 'And it all stopped. Do you suppose that was evil spirits leaving the place?'

'Perhaps. I don't know, Josh. All I do hope is that it means a new start for Juliet and Leo. They've had trouble enough as it is.'

A silence, until Rosalind had safely negotiated the bumpy track and they were out again on the main road; then Josh said, 'Mum, I've got myself a job—computer support, consultancy, that sort of thing. Sally Oldfield asked if I'd join her outfit some time ago. I emailed her last night to say yes.'

'I'm so glad! That's really good!'

'Hang on, though—that's not the whole story. I'm doing it to fund some further study. I want to do a course in theology. Just to explore things a bit more. After today, more than ever.'

Rosalind was so astonished she nearly drive the car off the road. 'Wow! That's not what I expected! Oh Josh, I'm so glad.' She grinned and glanced at her son. 'You can keep me up to date with the latest thinking!'

Tonight will tell, thought Juliet. Tonight she would sleep in her own bed, in her own room; the ultimate test of what Rosalind—or some agency acting through her—had done today.

That did not mean she was not afraid. She felt her heart thud, her mouth dry as she went into the bedroom and began to undress. She had brought Tiger with her, relieved that he was already turning and turning in the middle of the bed, kneading a comfortable hollow in the duvet. Leo had offered to sleep beside her, but rather to her own surprise, she had refused; and that in spite of the fact that she found herself longing to lie beside him again, to share the tenderness she had denied them both for so long. 'Not tonight,' she told him. 'Tomorrow night, if—if it's all right. But tonight—I think I need to face this alone.'

So he'd kissed her tenderly and left her. 'Just shout if you need me!'

She thought she would lie awake for hours, going over the events of the day in her mind, but in fact she fell quickly and deeply asleep. And then she dreamed—she knew this time that it was only a dream. At first, it seemed to be the same one she'd had on her first night at Holywell. She was looking down on the garden, seeing the lady walking among the low box hedging. She could smell the roses even from her vantage point at her open bedroom window; she could see them clearly too, exquisite blooms, fold after fold of petals, some fallen on the grassy paths along which the lady walked: Katharine Machyn, enjoying the tranquil beauty of her garden.

But this time she was not alone. There, running backwards and forwards, round and round, but always coming back to her, was a small child, a toddler with the drunken run of the very young, hampered a little by the long heavy skirts of infancy. A boy? A girl? Juliet couldn't tell. She only knew this was the lady's grandchild, and there was a strong tie of love between them. Happiness filled the garden, and the laughter of the child, dissolving to giggles as he ran to his grandmother and was caught up in her arms, lifted into the air, hugged and kissed. Over her shoulder he beamed at the world, raised his eyes to the window, and his blue gaze was on Juliet's.

Then they weren't blue any more, but brown, soft velvet brown eyes: Luke's eyes, her sweet, pink-cheeked child, her love, her darling…Not just the toddler Luke, all warm solid curves, laughter, sweetness, but Luke through all the unfolding years, Luke in his essence, the infant, the boy; the young man setting out on the adventure of life.

Then came his voice, right beside her, in the room, in her ear, that young man's voice she'd last heard as he called from the door, car keys in hand. *Just taking Katie for a spin, Mum! See you later!'* and then reassuring her that he was a good driver. *'We'll be fine!'*

Only this was not a call from afar, but a tender intimate voice, just behind her, as if he were standing as he used often to do with his arm about her shoulder. *'It's OK, Mum. Really!'*

She felt the consolation, the reassurance through every part of her. A deep peace seemed to flow along her veins, relaxing her limbs as if she rested on the softest of clouds, held, nestled, protected. *'It's OK.'* All was well. She could take a step, a first tentative step, into a future without grief or fear.

Then she came gradually, gently, to wakefulness—and knew, as so often in the early days following the accident, that what had happened in sleep, the way the world was put to rights while she dreamed, was an illusion. Luke was not at her side, telling her it was all OK.

What in heaven's name was 'OK' about anything? He had gone. She would never see him again. That moment of tenderness was just a dream, a cruel instant of wish-fulfilment.

And yet—and yet…

She opened her eyes on the room, bathed in the low morning sunlight of autumn, and found she was still cocooned in a sense of peace. He had gone. There was no escaping that dismal fact, no way out. But she knew suddenly that the Luke of her dream had been right: it *was* OK. Not good, not wonderful—just OK. There was a life before her that would for the most part be bearable, where sometimes even real happiness was possible, where she could laugh again; where she and Leo could hope to rediscover the love they once had for one another.

Not for them the joy of a grandchild, the sense of having a stake in the future, of long vistas reaching into generations to come. For them the only future was the littleness of what remained of their lives, a constricted space. They would simply have the time left to them, however short or long, and what they made of it for themselves alone. If there was an afterlife, where one day they might be reunited with Luke—Well, she would not allow herself to hope for that, still less believe. If it came, it would be a joy beyond imagining, but she was not going to constrict herself by hanging on to that unknowable possibility. What was here, now, from day to day, had to be enough.

Yet somehow she found that from being able only to face one day at a time, to endure what the moment held and no more, she believed that she would now be able to look on the coming days with hope, even to make plans, aiming to fill her life with what was useful and good and wholesome. Grief had not gone—it would be with her always, in some shape or form, ready to break into her tranquillity, to upset all her hard-won calm, a dark place at her heart for ever. No day would pass without thoughts of Luke. But now that she and Leo had broken through the barrier of their loss, and accepted that it was a shared loss, a shared grief, they could begin at last to learn to bear it together, as they shared the good things too.

The house for instance, as it took shape around them, renewed, restored, filled with their growing enjoyment; she was sure now that it would become completely, entirely, a place of peace. And there was the garden—*that* would be her task, to revive the loveliness she had glimpsed in her dreams. She lay quietly with eyes closed, imagining how it would look—the low box edging the beds, the old roses glowing, filling the air with their perfume, a place where she and Leo could walk and talk, or simply sit and enjoy a moment of tranquillity. She would find the right seat—a low stone seat perhaps— to put where she had seen one in her dream.

Today was a fine sunny day; she could see the light rimming the curtains. She would get dressed and go to work, taking up where she had left off. Never mind if Leo found out what she was doing; she no longer feared that she could not make him understand why she was doing it.

Then she remembered Katie, who was still her guest. For the first time, she found herself wishing (guiltily) that the girl was not there. She was glad that they were able to keep in touch, but she was beginning to accept that Katie had a new and different life ahead of her in which there would be little room for them. Still, Katie was here now and had to be considered. Perhaps today she would like to help with the gardening. If not, then Juliet would have to find some other way to entertain her.

There was a knock on the door, then it opened. 'Your breakfast, madam.' Leo was bearing a tray, with orange juice, coffee, a boiled egg, toast.

'Oh, you angel!' She sat up so Leo could put the tray on her lap. He perched on the end of the bed, picking up the kitten who was showing rather too close an interest in the buttered toast. 'I think it's time he came downstairs for his breakfast. Did you sleep well?'

'Wonderfully! The best night for months!' Then: 'Is Katie up?'

'Ah! Funny you should ask that! Yes, she's up,

but—I know you'll miss her, I know how you feel, but she's asked me to take her to the station, once you're up and she can say goodbye. She said she thought it was for the best. That we needed time to ourselves. I tend to think she's right.' He watched anxiously for her reaction, which was not quite what he'd expected.

'So do I. How sweet of her to be so considerate!'

Later, when she'd watched the car disappear into the distance, she went first, boldly, trying to keep fear at bay, towards the hall. She stepped in, crossed the flagged floor, opened the door on to the spiral stair. It smelt a little damp, the steps were worn, but that was all. And the arch above the door—Leo was right, it was beautifully carved, a fine example of craftsmanship. She ran her hand over it as Leo had done. Fear had left her completely.

She closed the door and went to dress in her old clothes; then took spade, fork, gardening gloves, pruners and wheelbarrow to the garden and set to work. For the first time in well over a year she felt a real lightness about the heart.

Finale

'I thought I'd find you here.'

Juliet looked round, startled. She hadn't heard the car or seen Leo emerge from the house. But there he was, watching her from the gate with an affectionate smile. She glanced at her watch: nearly one o'clock. She'd been here for hours—no wonder she felt hungry. 'I know I should be doing the plaster...'

'Too fine a day for that.'

She had cleared every last visible trace of weeds, turned and turned the soil with spade and fork. The dark earth smelt rich and good; excellent growing soil. As she'd worked, she'd seen the future garden take shape, exactly as she wanted it, the garden of her dream. All she needed now was the box hedging and the roses —and this was just the right time of year for planting them.

'I've got something for you.'

She rubbed earthy hands on her trousers and looked at him. She saw then that he was carrying something wrapped in sacking. 'For me? Why?'

'Because—' He paused, clearly considering his words; then, softly, 'Because I love you. And it's been hard, lately. For a long time, but especially lately.' He put the sacking down beside her. She saw pruned branches sticking out, thorny. 'Here we are then. Here's your old rose. *Rosa Mundi.* One of the oldest roses there is. I can't guarantee it smells exactly like your rose, but I hope it'll do.'

Juliet gazed at him, speechless because of the tears that rose in her eyes, choked in her throat.

'Aren't you going to plant it then?' He held up a packet. 'I've even got some rose food for it.'

She laughed. 'Oh—yes! Of course!'

She broke into frantic activity, digging a good deep hole, sprinkling rose food into it, watering. Then while Leo held the plant in place she covered the roots, firmed the soil with her feet. 'In Luke's memory. For the future, and the past too.'

'That's a bit metaphysical for me. Let's just say it's for us to enjoy, in our new home.' Then he took her in his arms and kissed her, and she knew it was going to be all right.

www.ingramcontent.com/pod-product-compliance
Lightning Source LLC
Chambersburg PA
CBHW061053190726
48286CB00006B/1736